About the author

Jesús Carazo was born in Burgos, Spain, and now lives in Bordeaux. He has published eighteen novels and twenty plays, winning many literary prizes. *El soñador furtivo* [*Furtive Dreamer*] was named one of the top 100 YA novels of the 20th century. His plays have been performed around the world. One of them, *Último verano en el paraíso* [*Final Summer in Paradise*], won Spain's most famous international award for dramatic literature, the *Lope de Vega* prize, in 2004.

The Chasms of the Night was awarded the prestigious *Ateneo-Ciudad de Valladolid* prize in Spain and has also been published in France.

THE CHASMS OF THE NIGHT

Jesús Carazo

THE CHASMS OF THE NIGHT

Translated by Zoe McNamee

Vanguard Press

VANGUARD PAPERBACK

© Copyright 2019
Jesús Carazo
Translated by Zoe McNamee

The right of Jesús Carazo to be identified as author of
this work has been asserted by him in accordance with the
Copyright, Designs and Patents Act 1988.

All Rights Reserved

No reproduction, copy or transmission of this publication
may be made without written permission.
No paragraph of this publication may be reproduced,
copied or transmitted save with the written permission of the
publisher, or in accordance with the provisions
of the Copyright Act 1956 (as amended).

Any person who commits any unauthorised act in relation to
this publication may be liable to criminal
prosecution and civil claims for damages.

A CIP catalogue record for this title is
available from the British Library.

ISBN 978 1 784656 61 4

*Vanguard Press is an imprint of
Pegasus Elliot MacKenzie Publishers Ltd.*
www.pegasuspublishers.com

First Published in 2019

**Vanguard Press
Sheraton House Castle Park
Cambridge England**

Printed & Bound in Great Britain

To Inés and Javier Guinard

"Where to, sir?" asked the coachman.

"Where you like," said Leon, forcing Emma into the cab.

And the lumbering machine set out. It went down the Rue Grand-Pont, crossed the Place des Arts, the Quai Napoleon, the Pont Neuf, and stopped short before the statue of Pierre Corneille.

"Go on," cried a voice that came from within.

The cab went on again, and as soon as it reached the Carrefour Lafayette, set off downhill, and entered the station at a gallop.

"No, straight on!" cried the same voice.

The cab came out by the gate, and soon, having reached the Cours, trotted quietly beneath the elm-trees. The coachman wiped his brow, put his leather hat between his knees, and drove his carriage beyond the side alley by the meadow to the margin of the waters.

It went along by the river, along the towing-path paved with sharp pebbles, and for a long while in the direction of Oyssel, beyond the isles.

But suddenly it turned with a dash across Quatremares, Sotteville, La Grande-Chaussee, the Rue d'Elbeuf, and made its third halt in front of the Jardin des Plantes.

"Get on, will you?" cried the voice more furiously.

And at once resuming its course, it passed by Saint-Sever, by the Quai des Curandiers, the Quai aux Meules, once more over the bridge, by the Place du

Champ de Mars, and behind the hospital gardens, where old men in black coats were walking in the sun along the terrace all green with ivy. It went up the Boulevard Bouvreuil, along the Boulevard Cauchoise, then the whole of Mont-Riboudet to the Deville hills.

It came back; and then, without any fixed plan or direction, wandered about at hazard. The cab was seen at Saint-Pol, at Lescure, at Mont Gargan, at La Rougue-Marc and Place du Gaillardbois; in the Rue Maladrerie, Rue Dinanderie, before Saint-Romain, Saint-Vivien, Saint-Maclou, Saint-Nicaise – in front of the Customs, at the 'Vieille Tour', the 'Trois Pipes', and the Monumental Cemetery. From time to time the coachman on his box cast despairing eyes at the public-houses. He could not understand what furious desire for locomotion urged these individuals never to wish to stop.

Gustave Flaubert, *Madame Bovary*
(Part III, Chapter I)

PROLOGUE

At the time of writing, three months have passed since the mysterious disappearance of Germán Altabella on 7th August 1994, in circumstances upon which the police have not yet been able to shed any light. For those unfamiliar with this eminent man of letters, let us just recall that he was born in our city forty-five years ago and that he has published two moderately successful novels: The Gates of Paradise *and* The Secret of the Shadows. *A research project and an ill-advised love affair kept him in France for many years, but after his return he became an integral part of our literary circle. Until recently, he divided his time between teaching French in a secondary school and his dual roles of critic and journalist.*

I met Germán Altabella shortly after moving to this city. We ran into each other at a busy tertulia, *a literary gathering held every Thursday in a small café on the Plaza Mayor. Our friendship was neither as intimate nor as profound as one might have supposed. Although G. A. may have seemed exceptionally affable to those who did not know him, he possessed an unpleasant vein of sarcasm and cruel irony: an electric fence which kept others at arm's length. From time to time, he would give me an article or a passage from one of his novels to study. He maintained that my position as a foreigner gave me a fresh perspective on literary matters. "Pallochi,* che*!" he would say, humorously imitating my Argentinian accent, "your point of view is so much more* lucid, *more* universal, *than that of us poor country bumpkins." I would petition him regularly for advice on my first novel,[1] and then on the second (to be published in a few months' time). Despite this, our relationship stayed within the bounds of the lively* tertulias *of the Plaza Mayor, where Altabella entertained everyone with demonstrations of his merciless wit.*

Several weeks after that fateful 7th August, I received a parcel containing a beautifully bound botanical work, The Anatomy of Plants *(1874). At first, I thought that there must have been a mistake; I barely speak French and, of course, have no interest in botany whatsoever. It was only when I started leafing through the pages that I discovered the following text, scrawled onto the back of the coloured plates in a fine, spidery hand. It presented itself as an account of the incredible circumstances of Germán Altabella's disappearance, written by the man himself. I'd already heard some discomfiting rumours about certain aspects of G. A.'s personality; this, and my familiarity with his writing style, would have convinced me of the document's authenticity, had the story itself not been so unhinged. The text lays Altabella's disappearance at the door of a*

---

[1] *The Echoes of Destiny*, Centaur Editions, 1990

certain Hilario Campillo, supposedly resident of a nearby village.

I will gloss over the troubling effect this discovery had upon me, and my rush to hand The Anatomy of Plants *over to the police. Unfortunately, this new line of enquiry has yet to bear fruit. On the one hand, the police graphologists still can't agree on the authenticity of the handwriting; on the other, Inspector Ceballos, the detective in charge of the investigation, suspects Altabella of one of those practical jokes favoured by men of letters. He has gone so far as to suggest that G. A. might reappear once this fantastic tale is published.*

The author of this prologue regrets that he is unable to share the inspector's optimism. It is true that all enquiries into Hilario Campillo have shed no light on the events; although we have found eight or ten people answering to this name in neighbouring villages, none of them has matched, either physically or temperamentally, the tormented individual described in the following pages. The waiters of the city café where Germán Altabella and Hilario Campillo supposedly had their second, fateful meeting, have been unable to help: they cannot even be certain of having seen our author on 7th August—although this is hardly surprising in such a busy establishment.

Perhaps we should work backwards and ask ourselves if Germán Altabella had any enemies. I have already mentioned his redoubtable sarcasm, which piqued both the tertulias *of the Plaza Mayor and his regular literary column in the local paper. He was not unlikely to have made some enemies among the authors who entered their manuscripts for local competitions, where G. A. often presided over the judging panel, or amongst those who had seen their creative efforts torn apart by our friend's scathing irony.*

Naturally, I have no desire to throw accusations around, but hope to contribute to the investigation as best I can, so that the mystery may be solved as quickly as possible.

While the enquiry is ongoing, and despite the continued uncertainty surrounding the identity of the account's author, G. A.'s publisher has decided to go ahead with the release. If he has entrusted me to transcribe the manuscript – a task that could have been carried out by any number of the author's close friends, and probably with greater expertise – it is doubtless because (to my great surprise) the pages were addressed to me. In any case, his choice does me honour and I have carried out this work fuelled by the friendship and respect that I have always felt for our illustrious colleague. Some readers will probably question the authenticity of the document, while others will perhaps accept it as the only explanation for an otherwise unfathomable disappearance. I hope that this tale will allow us, as best we can, to fill the painful and mysterious void that Germán Altabella has left among us.

Mario Pallochi
November, 1994

ONE

I have desired to write these pages, destined to traverse the great chasm of time, for a number of years. A fragile missive dependent upon the uncertain zeal of a carrier pigeon, I tremble to think that these pages may never reach you, dear reader, but if one day they should find themselves in your hands, spare a thought for their long and singular journey. I also fear that the story that they recount may seem improbable to you; I imagine you raising your eyebrows, ready to accept as truths such popular suspicions as Mario Pallochi has doubtless outlined in a painstaking and conscientious prologue. Alas (!) when this tale comes to light, I will no longer be in a position to answer them. Instead I must petition your wisdom and comprehension, at the same time soliciting your indulgence with regard to this convoluted nineteenth-century style to which, despite my stubborn resistance, my pen has finally succumbed.

At the time of the events to which I fell victim in the summer of 1994, I was an elegant man in my forties who earned a living through the writing of newspaper articles and the teaching of French in a secondary school. Prior to this, I had resided in France, where I had worked in an arts centre on the outskirts of Paris and, later, produced a thesis on Flaubert. When I returned to my country, I discovered that this time abroad had bestowed upon me a certain reputation as a cosmopolitan man of letters – a reputation which, I hasten to add, I did my best to cultivate.

My reviews and articles appeared regularly in the local press, and I can justly claim that I figured among the leading lights of the city's cultural life. My expertise would be called upon whenever there was question of presenting a book, giving a speech at a local festival or presiding over the judging panel of a literary award. Rarely would a week go by without my name or, as I said, my face appearing in a newspaper—on the occasion of a poetry competition, perhaps, or beaming with admiration beside one of the national treasures who occasionally passed through our historic city. My personal life, however, had not taken the same heady path. After a handful of lubricious but ill-fated love affairs, I found myself on the point of becoming one of those hardened bachelors, so often encountered in provincial towns, whose pathetic fate has them sneering at the few women with whom it would still be possible to build a lasting relationship, and pining after younger, more ardent specimens—those for whom, alas, they have long ceased to exist.

Once a week, our little circle of literary enthusiasts would hold, in an old café on the Plaza Mayor, one of those *tertulias* where it is customary to tear to shreds any person impudent enough to have published a book. I myself had written two novels some years before, which the local newspapers had greeted with a level of enthusiasm only matched by the resounding indifference of the national press. However, my fellow citizens read them with pleasure: a pleasure which I would reciprocate by inscribing the books with long, poetic dedications by the dozen.

I visited the public library every Tuesday in order to leaf through various cultural revues and newspaper supplements, searching therein for inspiration for my own articles (not to mention scraps of incendiary gossip to feed the flames at the next *tertulia*). It was during one of these visits that I happened to make the acquaintance of Hilario Campillo, the unlikely protagonist of this astonishing tale. One afternoon, Hilario sat opposite me at a reading table and scrutinised me through his thick glasses as though he had just read something terrible in the lines of my face. One might have said that he believed that a great disaster (a death in the family, a broken leg, a visit from the tax inspector) was sure to fall upon me as soon as I stepped out of the door. Attributing this individual's open curiosity to my status in the city, I endeavoured to concentrate on my work. To no avail, of course, for every time I raised my head to reflect on how best to exploit a particular subject in the literary domain, my eyes would meet those of Hilario, fixed resolutely on my face. I barely had the time to glimpse the round lenses of his spectacles, which cast a number of concentric circles upon a pair of unnerving, distorted pupils. I began to think that it was not the mere fact of sitting across from a local celebrity that made my neighbour gaze upon me with such impertinence and obstinacy. I decided to face him down. For four or five seconds, we froze, like two wild stags before a fight. Then, his face twisted with fear, and he whispered in a trembling voice:

"I read your novel."

I cannot but admit that this flattering opener wiped all traces of ferocity from my face.

"Which one?" I asked, mentally admitting him into my small but select circle of admirers.

"The Gates of... Paradise."

As always when someone tells me that they have read one of my novels, I hastened to sing the praises of the other title, *a much better read by all accounts*. Hilario promised to buy a copy and returned to showering me with compliments on the novel with which he was already familiar. Modesty prevents me from enumerating his comments on my mastery of rhythm and action, intense storytelling, character descriptions, realism, atmosphere, plot, and the tale's magnificent, unexpected dénouement[2]... Naturally, I agreed wholeheartedly with his opinion. Then the man fell silent again and I, faced once more with his fearful

---

[2] The reader should be patient and understanding when faced with these moments of authorial vanity. (Note: Mario Pallochi)

regard, felt for a moment like a prisoner in the electric chair gazing at his executioner. Eager to escape this discomfiting situation, I asked him about the book he was reading. He showed me the cover: it was a Ray Bradbury novel. He must have noticed my disgust because he asked me if I liked science fiction. I sneered: "Ah! If any genre deserves to be banned, it is that of science fiction." He seemed offended and admitted that he had written a few fantasy stories himself in the past. "You write, do you?" I asked, sensing in him an unexpected rival.

Hilario waved his hand, as if to waft away cigarette smoke.

"Just poems, short stories, pastiches of novels, that kind of thing," he murmured.

I asked his name and, without knowing exactly why, felt that this 'Hilario Campillo' was not unknown to me. When I enquired as to whether his work had already been published, he looked at me sharply (his expression one of eloquent horror), as though I were somehow responsible for his condition of unpublished author.

"I haven't been interested in that nonsense for a long time," he answered lugubriously.

As I was not greatly troubled by his words, even though his tone betrayed a degree of envy and disgust, I decided to take up the gauntlet. "I don't understand how a man of letters can enjoy such nonsense," I said, gesturing at the volume in his hands.

Hilario had not expected such a direct attack, and, after a short hesitation, he argued that novelists had the right to unbounded creativity, even flights of fancy. I immediately came out in support of literary realism and, as I naturally had greater knowledge of the subject than he, Hilario found himself fighting a losing battle. I remember that our exchange became more and more charged; the charming woman sharing our table, far from telling us to pipe down, actually began to spur me on, coming down firmly on the side of Galdós, Cervantes, Clarín and other great figures of Spanish literary tradition. Hilario, beside himself, quoted Cortázar and Borges, whilst I threw myself into a tortuous analysis of the differences between *plausible* and *unbridled* fantasy. I made a fairly passive-aggressive remark about the reputed immaturity of science-fiction readers. He refuted my arguments with an energetic shake of his head and his face, twisted in horror, betrayed an expression of desperate helplessness. Stammering and blushing, he appealed to our neighbour for support, but the young woman was insensible to his arguments, her face icier at each silent entreaty. I began to worry that Campillo would lose his composure and pounce upon me, and that we would end up rolling around on the library floor.

Our dispute was brought to an end as one might expect: someone at a nearby table told us to be quiet, my adversary pulled an angry face, and our lovely neighbour threw me a furtive, knowing glance. I felt as though I had won a moral victory. Then, fearing that the discussion might continue beyond the sacrosanct confines of the library, I waited until Hilario was busy blowing his nose into a grubby handkerchief, and slipped out.

Inexplicably, from that day onwards, I began to see him everywhere. I should add that each time we bumped into each other, he sped up; our greeting never went beyond a hasty, impersonal nod. Sometimes, he seemed to be a few steps ahead of me. I would go into the bank, book shop or post office just as he was leaving and notice a smug smile on his lips that in no way contradicted his usual timorous air. On other occasions, I would find him staring into a shop window, apparently absorbed in the contemplation of some incongruous object: an orthopaedic truss, a fitted kitchen or an advert for a popular brand of laxative. It was becoming difficult for me to go into town at all without encountering him, an elusive figure in a washed-out grey suit.

If two or three days went by without my seeing him (passing by my house or in the doorway of some public place), my heart would swell with the fragile hope that the harassment had finally come to an end. This would be accompanied by – I know not why – an insidious sense of malaise, brought about by the fear of bumping into Hilario, with his pitiful, terrified expression, yet again. Once or twice, I thought about confronting him to ask the point of this stupid surveillance campaign, but I quickly abandoned the idea; I could imagine his affected confusion, his blushing protestations and his insupportable, hypocritical excuses. Still in the dark as to the meaning of all this, I began to think of it as one of those ridiculous Oriental tortures which, subtly at first, intensifies to plunge its victim into an irreversible state of despair. As it was, after two or three weeks, this man knew everything about me: the route of my after-dinner walks, the time I finished my lessons, the name of my savings bank, my irresistible passion for pornographic magazines...

During the summer months, most of my friends being out of town, I had the habit of going, as the shadows lengthened, to a busy café. I enjoyed being surrounded by people. One day in early August, while I was leafing through a newspaper on the terrace of this establishment, I spotted Hilario near the counter. (I daresay I knew that I was going to see him even before the fact, much like those animals who can sense thunderstorms or earthquakes.) On this occasion, he did not look away as he had always done during our *accidental* meetings in the street; he gazed at me openly, his lips stretched thinly in a smile or semblance thereof. His eyes met mine for a few seconds, and the situation became so ridiculous and so uncomfortable that I gestured to him to take a seat at my table – but, at that very moment, one of those distant cousins who always turn up at inopportune moments appeared and sat down beside me. Hilario stopped short and turned on his heel. I hotly regretted my relative's interruption, but I now know that after all the twists and turns of his ignoble spying campaign, Hilario had finally decided to take the next step.

TWO

Every day for the next few days, I went to the same café, convinced that I would see him again. The reader must forgive me for having not yet described this place. Suffice to say that it was situated in a road in the heart of the city and that it had known a relative splendour in the 1960s, when the provincial bourgeoisie had held frequent meetings within its walls. But the establishment now seemed gripped by an inexorable decline. It was impossible to classify. The elegant silverware and tasteful upholstery of previous years had been replaced by others of doubtful taste, and the serving staff – doubtful too – distributed food and drinks with bad grace. I remember that, some afternoons, there floated in the air a familiar and inexorable sorrow that only we, the regulars, could identify.

It was on the 7th August 1994 that our man finally appeared and sat at my table. I know that it was nine o'clock because it was at that moment that a beeping watch made me look up from my newspaper, only to discover Hilario Campillo's insufferable face looking at me from the counter. At his feet was a large leather briefcase. I believe that, as before, we spent a few seconds gazing at each other before I invited him to join me. Hilario accepted with a smile, picked up his briefcase and his little cup of coffee, and slowly made his way across the room. By the time he got to me, more than half of his coffee had spilled into the saucer. He seemed preoccupied. He sat opposite me and, contemplating the disaster with an air of unutterable astonishment, apologised as though it had been my drink, rather than his own.

This was followed by a long silence—one of those embarrassing, tense silences which floated around Hilario like bubbles of repressed eloquence. Perhaps his hesitancy meant that he did not yet wish to reveal the mysterious reason that had pushed him to pursue me for several weeks. I decided to give him some time.

"Are you sure you don't mind my joining you?" he asked suddenly. His tone was unexpectedly timid.

"Just as long as you promise not to talk to me about science fiction…" I joked.

Hilario blushed, then cleared his throat twice as though preparing to give a long speech.

"I promise… of course," he replied, his face gradually returning to its usual pale pink.

"I can't deny that I've been waiting to meet with you for several days now."

"To be honest… I didn't dare interrupt you," he said apologetically. "I've always believed that a writer's imagination never… relents. Even as we speak, perhaps… uh… perhaps you're planning the next chapter of your new novel."

"Sorry to disappoint you, but there is no new novel. It's been a long time since I've had any ideas worth sacrificing the next two years of my life for."

"Just a dry spell, surely," he replied ingratiatingly, as though forcing himself to be amiable.

"Dry spell? Christ in the desert, more like!" I exclaimed, affecting the cynical nonchalance of Blasco Ibañez in his luxurious villa on the French Riviera.

Hilario looked at me for a moment, not knowing how to interpret my outburst. I feared he was about to blow across the table another of his elastic silences, but instead he continued:

"I hope you'll find a new subject soon and publish another book…"

"Maybe we'll read one of your own before then."

Hilario stared at me in horror. "*You already have*," he said coldly. "A literary competition sponsored by the building society."

"I say! I don't remember…" I babbled, wondering which of the hundreds of stories that I, as a member of the jury, had been obliged to read, could have come from the pen of this worrying individual.

"Of course, you do," replied Hilario, trying to jog my memory. "A short story, eight pages long, *The Eyes of the Labyrinth*…"

I smiled dumbly, without knowing what labyrinths his accursed story could possibly have been talking about.

Hilario continued: "An unpublished author who, looking at his bookshelves, remembers how his passion for literature has plunged him into the most terrible sense of despair. And at the end..." He repeated himself, as though prompting me to finish the phrase: "At the end..."

"Perhaps I didn't get around to reading it," I said gently, feeling a little guilty.

"You read it, Altabella. Of course, you did. At the end, crushed by his failure to publish a single novel, the protagonist sets fire to his collection and perishes in the flames, a victim of his own *incendiary* passion."

It was only when Hilario spelt out the ending that I suddenly remembered a turgid, sinister tale, a pale imitation of the fantasy writing of Borges.

"A magnificent piece of work!" I exclaimed.

"I suspect you did not think that at the time," Hilario said grudgingly. "I was led to believe that you'd personally refused to include me the shortlist."

What the devil...! I nodded my head as though prepared to accept the blame, all the while furiously wondering which nasty little spy on the jury could have passed on such information.

Hilario squinted distortedly at me through his glasses. "Apparently, the rest of the panel found my story perfectly acceptable."

Finding myself in a tight spot, I hastened to agree with the rest of the panel.

"I must admit that I developed a certain animosity for you, when I heard about it."

"Literary history is bursting at the seams with hasty judgements and grotesque mistakes," I replied. I endeavoured to make myself sound as apologetic as possible, despite feeling certain that there had been no error in this instance. In any case, I had never enjoyed judging the work of others, finding it an unpleasant and arrogant task.

"For a while," continued Hilario, "You were my only obstacle in this nasty, backward city."

I took a gulp of my gin and lemonade, which was beginning to get warm. "You can't be serious."

"You had everything a writer could have wanted: your photo in the papers, influence over the judging panels, the friendship of the authors who come here. I won't pretend I didn't envy you that," said Hilario.

"A healthy envy, I presume," I replied, trying to lighten the mood.

"Healthy? No. I was jealous—bitterly, obsessively jealous."

I laughed nervously: "But Hilario, I'm only a paltry provincial critic!"

He looked at me coldly: "For two years you were also editor of the Sunday poetry supplement in the local paper. Over those twenty-four months, I sent you the totality of my poetic output, under various imaginative pseudonyms."

I gasped. "So, it was you who, week after week…"

"Yes. I was *Simón de Simón* and *The Old Nostalgic*. Not to mention *Calliope*, *The Witless Ewe* and *Fabrice del Dongo*.

I remembered the poems. I had had only to read a few lines from any of them to discover, beneath the amusing pen names, the same unknown, bull-headed writer.

"Believe me, I'm very sorry—" I said, raising my glass to my lips again.

Hilario cut me off:

"You've got nothing to be sorry for. Maybe my poems didn't deserve any better."

"So, your work was never published!" I exclaimed, feigning regret.

Hilario gazed at the wall behind me as though I were both invisible and inaudible. Then he squeezed his coffee cup hard, his right hand suddenly tensing.

"It was, once," he continued sadly. "You printed a naïve, sentimental sonnet I had written as a teenager. *'In my arms, the spring of dreams...'*"

"I remember," I said hastily, cutting him off before he could go any further (I found poetry fairly dull, to tell the truth). "A magnificent poem!"

"A terrible poem!" said Hilario. "I was convinced that it wouldn't be published either."

"You were wrong," I said encouragingly.

"The worst part was finding it in the paper, printed with care, the following Sunday. It meant that my work hadn't improved a whit in twenty years."

"That's rather dramatic!"

"Dramatic, perhaps. But it allowed me to become more circumspect about my creative offerings."

Hilario sank into one of his sustained silences and looked me straight in the eye in that unsettling way. How many times must he have imagined my being struck by lightning or falling victim to an incurable disease! How many times must he have pictured my drowning in a stormy sea, or being consumed by flames in my own library, like the hero of his horrible story! Perhaps he had considered *taking matters into his own hands*. It was possible, I thought with a shudder, that the irritating surveillance campaign of the previous few weeks had been undertaken with the sole aim of bringing an end to my poor provincial life.

"I'm happy to say that I gave up the reins of that silly little supplement a long time ago," I said, trying to avoid Hilario's menacing stare.

"As for me, I haven't shown a single poem to anyone since that day," he replied. "12th February, 1989."

He pronounced the date effortlessly, as though he repeated it to himself several times per day as a kind of penance. He seemed to choose his words in an effort to make me feel guilty. He wouldn't succeed, of course. He was just one of countless readers to send their insipid love poems to the paper—just one of many. One could only hope that, for the greater good, all had since given up the pleasures of verse.

THREE

Hilario leaned towards me over the table and smiled with an air of vague melancholy.

While the lukewarm smile tried to conquer the fear hidden in his eyes, I could not escape the feeling that his features had changed. One might have said that the last few minutes of our conversation had transformed him, subtly and incrementally, into a stronger, shrewder being. Perhaps the insecurity that radiated from his person was little more than a mask. I wondered whether, in this old-fashioned café, he would reveal his true face to me at last.

"I won't lie to you," Hilario continued. "At first, I was overwhelmed by spite—I wrote a number of letters to the paper, insulting you and your poetry supplement in the vilest of terms. I called you a 'ridiculous bigwig', a 'vain scarecrow' and the poetry section a 'dung heap of old rhymes'.

I recall that his words left me feeling perplexed and, for a few moments, I didn't know how to react to Hilario's irritating show of sincerity.

"No offence, I hope," he said.

I shook my head and ordered another gin and lemonade from a passing waiter. Hilario did not want anything. A little coffee remained in his cup and he took a tiny sip every so often, as though intending to make it last all night.

"I shouldn't have told you about all these horrible things," he said contritely.

"Don't torture yourself, Hilario: I already knew about the letters," I lied. "The editor of the paper took great pleasure in forwarding them to me."

"That's odd—I always took steps to make them seem as though they hadn't come from the same person. I even copied different styles of handwriting, hoping that it would look like the whole city was turning against your column."

"In general, newspaper readers couldn't care less about poetic disputes."

Hilario shook his head thoughtfully: "You may be right." Suddenly, his tone brightened, and he leaned towards me, as though to tell a secret. "Do you know what the strangest part was? I actually took great pleasure in writing those letters. I felt as though I were bringing those imaginary correspondents to life... What started off as an act of revenge became an enjoyable obsession. I quickly abandoned my original project and started writing other letters on all sorts of subjects. I invented unusual complaints, terrible injustices, incredible accidents... One day, it was an old lady swallowed up by a drain; another day, a pedestrian chased by a canary or harassed by a lustful policeman. You see? That was how I discovered my passion for hoaxes, pastiche, confusing people."

"However did you find the time to indulge in this… manic letter-writing?"

"I must admit that I'm reasonably lucky in that sense. My parents left me a house in the country and a modest income which allows me to subsist, in my own frugal way (you can see the state of my suit and shirt) without the irritating obligations of gainful employment. It's true that my stipend shrinks alarmingly each year, but I cut back on my expenses, my needs… I'm able to – I mean, I *was* able to – live on very little…"

Hilario fell back into silence, as though swept away by some powerful, dark thought.

"And you're still writing these letters?" I asked him, eyeing him as an entomologist might contemplate a new specimen.

"Oh no, that all finished two years ago. One day, I realised that – if you'll forgive me – I had lost all respect for the living, and that it was high time I turned my attention to the dead."

This time, it was I who inched towards Hilario, seized by the disturbing confession that I felt lay behind his words. I think he caught my sudden curiosity because he smiled once more, his lips curving upwards while his eyes remained clouded with fear.

"I don't know what you're thinking," he said, looking around with an expression of anguish, "but I was alluding to the greatest writers of all time, our most illustrious ancestors. I wanted to pull from the jaws of death these authors' heroes: all those fascinating literary characters who, at one time or another, had made me laugh or cry. This desire drove me to write another ending to Romeo and Juliet (one in which the young lovers lived happily ever after until the age of a hundred), then to do the same for Ophelia and Hamlet. I also spared Macbeth his life (the Macbeths of this world always enjoy a peaceful dotage, I find). I won't hide from you, Altabella, that I was greatly proud of some of these changes."

"What an unusual idea!" I exclaimed, leaning back in my chair. I scanned the room for someone to rescue me.

"A game, if you like. But isn't all literature just that?"

I tried to avoid answering, and fired back with my own question, much less rhetorical:

"Why are you telling me all this?"

"I haven't told you anything yet!" Hilario replied. "You've no idea of the forces that have driven me, these past few weeks, to follow so closely your life, your movements, and to—"

"—to tail me, like a criminal?"

"You noticed that?"

"Of course I did."

"But I always made sure that our meetings seemed…" he hesitated, searching for the correct word: "…*fortuitous*."

"I didn't believe that for a minute."

"I'm sorry if I frightened you."

"You didn't *frighten* me in the slightest, Hilario; it was rather irritating, this spying game."

"I just wanted to know if you were trustworthy."

"Can you please stop speaking in riddles and come to the point?" I interrupted him impatiently, noting that it was almost ten o'clock.

Hilario's ears reddened to a surprising glow.

"One day," he continued, upping the pace, "I decided to take my redemptive project a step further. It was no longer a question of sparing the lives of literature's most famous characters, but of actually intervening at the crucial moment where their fates hang in the balance. I undertook a much more delicate, much more exciting project: one which compelled me to seek out those few barely perceptible textual fault lines into which I could introduce my own pen to pull my heroes from the jaws of tragedy. This I did with Sorel in *The Red and the Black*, Raskolnikov in *Crime and Punishment*…"

"And which of these two novels would you like me to read?" I asked him abruptly, hoping to bring this fanciful conversation to a close.

"Oh no, I don't wish to make you read any of my – *our* work," said Hilario. He seemed slightly offended. "I just want to give you an idea of the moment where

35

everything changed—that pivotal day where I found myself at the heart of an event that you'll surely want to dismiss as impossible and absurd."

This tortuous approach to storytelling was driving me to distraction. One could have said that, instead of moving forward in his narrative, Hilario was making any number of mysterious detours, each of which was casting us ever further adrift from its conclusion.

"You're never going to tell me, I suspect," I replied with an audible sigh.

"Patience, please!" continued Hilario, apparently unmoved by my testiness. "I am going to tell you about the extraordinary moment when I decided to redeem that poorest, most desperate, most piteous character: Emma Bovary."

I recall being suddenly flooded with indignation upon hearing that name. While writing my thesis in France in the 1970s, I had been obliged to read and reread the novel so many times that its heroine had become part of the fabric of my most intimate memories. I daresay that, at a time when I found real women fatally disappointing, Emma had become to my eyes as fascinating as she was inaccessible. Beneath the skin of a provincial, bourgeois housewife, she was volcanic. I would dream of her often—dream of holding her in my arms. Even upon waking, I would continue to live out my tumultuous fantasies of this sensuous free spirit, this liberated woman; a pleasure doubtless shared by any number of *Madame Bovary*'s many readers. That night in the café, hearing her name on Hilario's lips gave me a horrid feeling of violation, as though the memory of a first love had been soiled.

"So you dared—with Emma!" I exclaimed, unable to conceal my anger.

"Why shouldn't I have dared? Let's not forget that she dreamt of flying *'like a bird'* from Yonville, of *'growing young again somewhere far out in the stainless purity of space'*. To save her from the suffocating routine that was draining the life from her, I had to carve for her a new, exalted existence. I was convinced that such an act would in no way contradict Emma's own wishes."

"And the wishes of Gustave Flaubert, what of those?"

"Do let me go on. I've already told you that I have no respect for writers —those old, dead monsters. One winter night, I decided to carry out my heretical rescue mission by focusing on the passage in which she and Leon race through the streets of Rouen in a carriage, borne as it were on the wings of their burgeoning passion… You'll agree, surely, that she needed to be separated from her new lover, the man who was to prove her downfall…"

"I imagine you found it funny, snatching her away from the poor young clerk at such an inopportune moment."

Hilario ignored my jibe. He half-closed his eyes and started to speak again, this time very quietly, as though swept up in a mass of unforgettable pleasures: "It was as if I'd cut the bounds of a creature who was not only alive but palpitating with desire. For the first time, I felt that I was committing an act of sacrilege, but I could no longer refrain from doing so. My profane pen described how Emma threw herself from the carriage and hurtled through space and time, tearing through borders and centuries to join me here."

"All in a day's work!" I exclaimed, still wondering how to extricate myself from this outlandish conversation.

"Please let me speak. Now, this is the most extraordinary thing. While I was writing all this down, feverishly putting pen to paper in an upstairs room at home, I glanced through the window. Who should I see standing at the gate but a young woman. She was pale and beautiful—an altogether *old-fashioned* type of beauty, I thought. Her clothes were equally anachronistic (though these days, I admit, one never can tell). Her hair was in disorder and she seemed confused and hesitant, like someone arriving late after having lost their way. Something compelled me to put down my pen and go into the garden; when I approached her to ask if she needed any help, she smiled at me – a slow, lingering smile – then stammered a few words in French."

"Emma Bovary, the one and only!" I jibed.

Once again, Hilario seemed not to hear me.

"I remember very clearly inviting her in," he continued, "and she turned to me like a sleepwalker. I was feeling more and more nervous and I couldn't stop trembling. My hand, brushing against her shoulder, received what felt like a sudden electric shock. Once inside, I looked into her black eyes…"

"… which *pierced your heart like vine shoots*," I interrupted with Rodolphe's well-known phrase.

"I hope you won't laugh if I agree with you there. It was exactly like that," said Hilario. His voice was confidential, candid. "The strange woman sat down and gazed at me without a word. It was as though she were observing everything without great surprise, having found all as expected. When I asked her name, she thought for a long moment, then shook her head and began reeling them off: *Berthe*, *Amanda*, *Louise*… Then she shrugged, muttering something like "I've forgotten my memory". She didn't say that she'd *lost* her memory, but that she'd *forgotten* it. I think we spent at least a quarter of an hour just gazing at each other, while I tried to recall phrases from that language that I'd learnt at school so many years ago. Then I noticed that her eyelids were heavy, and that she was struggling to keep them open…"

I admit that Hilario's story was beginning to worry me; I couldn't imagine what he was looking for, what he stood to gain from inflicting his grotesque fantasy on me. Back then, of course, my perception of the world rested on a number of scientific certainties, much like the piers of a bridge, under which flowed the shadowy waters of mystery and religion. The reader can well imagine the sceptical smile with which I surveyed those rushing waves.

Hilario continued, enthralled: "When I noticed that she was on the brink of sleep, I offered her a room for the night. She accepted immediately and collapsed onto the bed, falling into a deep but restless slumber…"

"… but the following morning," resignedly I interrupted him again, raising my eyebrows mockingly, "the mysterious woman had disappeared."

"Not a bit of it. The next morning, she was still asleep and the rest of the day as well. I needn't tell you how anxious I was, nor how my anxiety grew as the day wore on without her emerging from the bedroom." Hilario paused dramatically. "Then, as night fell, she finally appeared in the doorway, groggy and listless. That was when I saw how attractive she was – her figure, her face – and how delicious her lips were. We had supper together in near-total silence and, at the end of the meal, I decided to utter a single word—a name, that of the last person that she had seen in her world. "*Leon*," I murmured, as she was biting into an apple. The fruit fell from her hands. "*Leon…*" she repeated, and two tears brimmed from her large black eyes, which *'seemed to hold successive layers of colour'*…"

"*'…darkest at the depths and growing brighter and brighter towards the surface'*," I continued, recognising the phrase. "And you want me to believe all this?"

"I couldn't believe it either, at first."

"Unfortunately for you, Hilario, literary heroes can only live in the mind of their reader."

"Oh, but I told myself the same thing! I told myself that it was impossible, and yet...!" he exclaimed, watching me through his thick glasses; I felt as one caught in the crosshairs of two menacing periscopes. "But do let me go on. After those tears (the cause of which seemed clearer to me than to her), my guest shrugged her shoulders, smiled sadly and continued to eat her apple. I believe that there was something symbolic, some defining moment in that episode—what I mean is that whilst she cut the fruit into little pieces and brought them delicately to her lips, I got the impression that she had accepted this unexpected change in her life, and perhaps even... (I hardly dared state it in words, even in my head) ... perhaps she had even accepted *me*. Because there was, in this brave resignation, the happy promise of other nights, of other evenings like that one, coming up on the horizon to lend the scene a character that was not only familiar, but verging on routine."

Hilario said nothing for a while. He rubbed his hand against his hollow cheeks, hoping to see, I imagine, the effect that the tale was having on his listener. I must admit that what had caught my attention was not the outright extravagant character of the reported facts, but Hilario's skill at drawing me gradually into the narrative of his imaginary adventure. By this point in our conversation, I had already started to suspect Hilario of wishing merely to give me the synopsis of a novel—one that he was writing, perhaps; or one that he would write if given my approval. I hoped that, upon reaching the end of the story, he would admit the truth and apologise for his deception.

"Well, get on with it," I pressed him, hoping to break the irritating silence which had fallen between us. For the first time, I watched the movement of his lips.

"That evening, we were able to exchange a few phrases at most. She wanted to know my name and, upon hearing it, she said it was funny. She repeated it clumsily: *Hilaguio, Hilaguio.* Then she admitted that she was very tired and wanted to go back to her room. As she stood up to leave, she stroked my hair and smiled. It was neither the touch of a ghost nor the pale tepidness of a moonbeam..." Hilario raised his eyebrows, like the two arches of a bridge. He continued: "The following days were, for us, a slow and careful series of discoveries, enlivened by conversations peppered with amusing, sometimes grotesque, misunderstandings. Fortunately, Emma's horizons were already filling with various domestic projects: tablecloths, curtains, embroidered runners and antimacassars... It seemed as though she were forcing herself into activity: as though she feared the full weight of the past – obsessive, unbearable – falling upon her shoulders at the first quiet moment. Every so often I would buy her a dress or a blouse that she would try on with astonished delight. She said that she felt half-naked in such apparel... One day she sat at the old piano that I had inherited from my grandparents and, from that day onwards, she spent every morning there, tapping out tunes that I didn't know. We even went into town together, and one of the most delicious moments of our time together remains to me that of her innocent, smiling astonishment at the sight of lit-up shops, cars, traffic lights. The absence of horses surprised her more than anything: "*where are the horses?*" she asked me again and again. She didn't understand how these horrible four-wheeled monsters could have replaced such a docile, beautiful animal. When it was time to go home, she stood gazing sadly at the thin river, caught up in nostalgia, and I felt something terrible and indescribable rear up between us. It seemed as though at any moment the utterance of a magic spell, the mere wave of a hand, would make her disappear. I would often call her over from the other side of the house, just to make sure that she was still there…"

While Hilario laid out his delusions, his face took on the tortured, confused wince of a victim. I took pains to remind myself that he was just outlining one of his senseless novels and that he wanted to test (on a receptive and sensitive reader, of course) a plotline that was not only unrealistic, but absurd.

"I fear that you may have forgotten an essential part of the narrative," I said, seizing upon one of his sporadic silences.

Hilario hoisted his thick black eyebrows yet further up his forehead. (They seemed to me on the point of falling into his coffee cup.)

"I don't understand," he replied.

"Well, what about the *volcanic passion* that must engulf the writer and his mysterious visitor? I suppose you've thought of that?"

"Ah! *that…*" he said, stretching his neck as though his crumpled tie were beginning to choke him. "I don't know if I should talk about *that…*"

"Of course, you should! That kind of thing interests everyone!"

I remember that as he listened to my advice, he nodded several times, slowly and reflectively, without so much as opening his mouth. I suspected that he hadn't thought of it. Perhaps he was a timid, prudish writer, despite his sacrileges and profanities.

"These days, a novel that draws a veil over such things is going to alienate half its—"

"But I'm not talking about a novel!"

"I know, I know," I conceded, "but I find that part of the story very interesting."

Hilario gulped down the remainder of his coffee; then he clenched his hands together with a show of contained strength. I had the impression that my pursuit of this line of discussion was making him uncomfortable.

"We soon became… lovers, if that's what you want to know," he said. "She was terribly attractive, despite having none of the… *exuberance* of modern women. I mean that she…" Hilario searched for the words and almost choked on them: "I mean that she didn't drape herself about provocatively like a film star, or a television actress. Flaubert, as you know, didn't give us much detail on the sexuality of his heroine, but I can assure you that our nights together, our nights of passion and debauchery were just..." He sighed, unable to describe the scene, and let his sentence go unfinished. "From that day onwards, I *consecrated* myself entirely to her. An old-fashioned word, I know, but I can't describe in any other way my soul's fervent desire to please her. Would you believe me, Altabella, if I told you that I even tried to dream up new, extravagant treats in order to satisfy her senseless penchant for novelty and wastefulness? I've already mentioned that I only have a few assets which allow me to live on a modest income, but during this time I decided to spend everything on her. I bought her jewellery, hats, shoes; I would hold the mirror so that she could look at herself from every angle; I would listen for hours to the old melodies she performed on the piano (she was only a mediocre player, I admit). From time to time, I'd catch myself gazing at her with a dumb smile on my face and, suddenly self-conscious, I'd wonder what she thought of the man who grinned at her so ridiculously. I think that, weakened by the destructive effects of a lover's passion, I ended up as a second Charles Bovary."

"An unexpected and terrible fate!" I exclaimed mockingly, if only to remind him that I still didn't believe a word of his incredible tale.

Hilario didn't seem concerned. Perhaps he failed to see the irony in my comment. He looked at me as though from a great distance. His eyes seemed to be trapped beneath the round, foggy lenses of his glasses, which glimmered in the dusty light of the café.

"As soon as I recognised that I was playing the lamentable role of the complacent, entranced husband," he continued, "I felt the first gnawings of an unspeakable anguish: was I to share the fate of Flaubert's miserable cuckold? I must admit that this troubling uncertainty very quickly polluted the best parts of our relationship. Of course, I couldn't go through such a thing with the candour of my unfortunate predecessor. I knew too much and that was why I found myself obliged to be constantly on my guard, attentive to the slightest sign of impending disaster… Though afraid to confirm my suspicions, I would secretly scrutinise her face; I thought I could make out, in every melancholy silence, the terrifying phantom of betrayal. Although no neighbour ever visited me – I don't make friends with people just because they happen to live nearby – I started to sense a rival in the postman, the grocery deliveryman, the meter readers… This went on until the day of the unfortunate incident with the piano tuner…"

FOUR

"Emma often complained about the piano," continued Hilario, eyes fixed on his coffee-flooded saucer, "the old instrument upon which she played those lovely tunes, filling our home with the ghosts of days gone by, distant childhood memories, and, perhaps, impossible happiness. It was out of tune, and occasional flat notes marred her melancholy recitals a little. One day, she asked me if I could find someone in town who would allow her to practise on their piano for a couple of hours every week. I shivered, remembering Emma Bovary's 'piano lessons' in Rouen—her pretext for meeting her lover. Fearing that history might repeat itself, I decided to employ someone to tune our old Gaveau. And that was how a certain quiet young man, the piano-tuner, came to our home. That morning, I was supposed to go into town for a rather delicate appointment at the bank. I know that I could have postponed the outing, but I'd always trusted musicians. And that young man seemed so serious and so absorbed in his work, even when I had left the house and was getting into my car... I remember spending an hour at the bank; I was chatting with one of the clerks when I was suddenly struck by panic. It was completely irrational, of course, this unbearable anguish brought on by the memory of some chapters of Flaubert, but still: what if a cursed piano could have encouraged his protagonist's infidelities? I ended up rushing out of the bank and driving home, covering the few kilometres that separated us at breakneck speed. When I opened the front door, both of them were hunched over the piano, very close to each other and a little confused, their faces purple with shame. At least, that's what I thought I saw; perhaps it was only my own anguish that made me perceive them thus. The young man left straight away, after having charged me a derisory sum for the work (which in itself seemed suspect—suddenly, every new detail was like an alarm bell). Emma saw him to the garden gate and I stayed inside, devoured by jealousy, feeling more confused and helpless than ever…"

The gin must have been working, because I asked him bluntly: "And what happened next?"

Hilario smiled for a fraction of a second, almost without moving his lips, as though holding back a secret outburst of joy.

"That evening," he continued, a tragic catch in his voice, "I begged Emma to play me something on the freshly-tuned piano, but she refused, claiming to have a migraine. Ditto for the next day, and the days that followed; she was always too tired or not in the mood. Perhaps she had started to lose interest in the piano. Then, one night, I discovered the real reason for this sudden incomprehensible apathy. Emma had gone up to bed and I was in the living room, pensive and haunted by gloomy premonitions. I don't know why I did it, but I lifted the lid of the piano and ran a single finger over the old keys. I tapped out a slow scale, then stopped suddenly: there was a discord. A lightning bolt, a shot in the chest couldn't have matched the effect of that note! My heart pounding, I went through the keys again, pressing each of them in turn. Once unmasked, each flat note seemed to mock me. I wanted to burst into Emma's room, to beat her, to throw her out into the street. I spent the rest of the night torturing myself by imagining what must have happened: flirtation, laughter, kisses... I pictured them rolling around on the living-room carpet as we had done, she and I, the first time... I felt so pitiful, so pathetic."

Hilario, his courage failing, paused and I had to refrain from opening my mouth or in any way falling into the insidious trap that his silence offered me.

"I decided never to speak of the incident," he continued, raising his monstrous eyebrows. "I felt as though talking about it would only make me seem ridiculous and reduce me in her eyes. After all, I had deserved it. I knew the workings of this woman's soul. I knew better than Emma her base and shameful instincts. From that night onwards, nothing was the same. But I wasn't the only one whose attitude had changed: Emma also became more capricious and moody. One day, she insisted on having the living-room walls repapered in a dark, striped pattern not really to my taste. I understood that she was seeking the presence of other men in the house and watched her like a hawk during the decorators' visit. Then, one day… One day… I did something mad—something unforgivable."

"You killed her?"

"No, no. I managed to complicate things even more." He sounded afflicted, exhausted; I felt for him. With his left hand, Hilario tried to replace his cup in the coffee-filled saucer. He continued to speak without raising his head, like a child forced to admit a misdeed. "I hadn't written a word since Emma's arrival. I suppose you can understand that? I was terrified of… *making the same mistake.* But the awful situation in which I found myself pushed me towards another 'literary experiment', and I soon couldn't resist the temptation of reawakening the strange power that had surged through my pen with Emma. One afternoon, I decided to try another of these inexplicable reincarnations with a charming character who had always fascinated me: Dolores Haze."

"Who?"

"Dolores Haze," repeated Hilario. "Nabokov's *Lolita.*"

"For God's sake! Aren't you going a bit far?" I replied, anticipating the narrative consequences of this new folly.

"Yes. I believe I went too far." Hilario spoke as one who, at heart, was quite satisfied at having provoked a domestic catastrophe.

This was certainly the moment when I realised, with frightening certainty, that Hilario Campillo was insane.

It crossed my mind that his hare-brained story was not so much the plot of a novel as that of an unhinged psychodrama in which I was to play, despite myself, the role of therapist.

"You have read the book, I suppose?"

"Yes, I've read it. It's one of the best, most perceptive novels to come out of this century of violence and madness," I retorted, satisfied with my pithy, print-worthy *réplique*.

"I had read it several times and I admired the lucid irony of the author as much as the perverse charm of the protagonist."

"I don't think Lolita is the kind of character that's easy to love," I said, purely to contradict him.

Hilario nodded. "You have no idea how right you are. The only thing that interests this child is provocation, titillation, toying with the desire of others. Not to mention that she is trivial, malicious and fickle. However, given my fix with Emma (I mean by that my domestic situation), don't you agree that it would have been riskier to conjure up a grown woman? An adolescent could burst into our lives without arousing suspicion, but not an adult.

"You're rather... sick," I said, wagging my finger but prepared to play the therapist until the end of our session.

Hilario smiled like a mischievous child.

"Isn't everyone? Now, imagine my excitement that afternoon. I was sitting at my desk, Nabokov's novel open before me; I had made up my mind to kidnap another young person, to conjure another character out of thin air. I was sure that if I could find the key passage in the book, the words would once again act like a black hole... Nevertheless, the results of my second attempt were less immediate and less impressive than the first. I had to deliver a pitched battle against my own writerly inadequacies, each new push ending in failure and forced retreat. Something in the mysterious alchemy of words escaped me. At first I wanted to save Lolita at the start of the book, when the protagonist's *'simian eyes'* light upon her for the first time, half-naked and fascinating, on the *piazza* behind her house. In vain, I attempted to rewrite the passage where Humbert collects her from the summer camp and discovers a curious *'wan'* look on his nymphet's freckled face. Another failure. Next, I tried to intervene in the *'Party with Boys'*, where the protagonist monitors the group's decorum by coming downstairs for his pipe or paper every ten or twenty minutes. Again, nothing happened. I don't need to tell you that throughout my writing attempts, while I was forcing the worrisome teenager onto planes and ships, buses and trains in the direction of my home, I kept glancing outside in the hope of seeing her appear there, near the door, like Emma... But the road remained deserted, the garden silent and empty. It took me more than ten attempts to snatch her from the grasp of Humbert Humbert. And only then did I discover (purely by chance, of course) the unimaginable detail without which it would never have been possible to…"

Hilario left the sentence unfinished and raised his head to stare into my eyes. His own were two tunnels of fog. He must have anticipated the question that played on my lips, but I seized the opportunity afforded by his silence to glance around us. Only two tables were occupied within the café and they were at the other side of the room, pushed against a wall upon which were hanging a number of horrible paintings by a local artist: dark, disturbing, apparently cursed.

"I must remind you that you are the first person in whom I have confided," continued Hilario. His tone was reproachful, as though offended by my apparent lack of curiosity. "I don't even know if this feat can be brought about by… just anyone. In any case, there's only one trick to it. It all depends on the moment of the *second author's* intervention in the story: the precise instant at which his sacrilegious pen opens up the hinterland between two phrases and summons forth, like an invasive plant species, a new, living text—viscous, slow-growing, its tendrils gripping the edges of the chasm… It is through this space that the victim throws themselves into another part of this astounding universe… You'll recall that I dragged Emma from Leon's arms at the moment of their meeting in that carriage, its perplexed coachman driving them round and round the streets of Rouen. What they did in that vehicle, Flaubert leaves to the reader's imagination. Now, *listen*: the second time around, I was unsuccessful until it occurred to me to try the same thing with Lolita at a similar moment. I decided to intervene when the girl and the protagonist made love in that small Briceland hotel, populated principally by old ladies and clerics. Perhaps there is no conclusion to be drawn from this coincidence, but I am certain that therein lay the key to these stupefying materialisations, the essential departure point without which no such feat would have been possible. I have often wondered about the nebulous power of sex, its role in such stories... Perhaps we can attribute all to those few seconds of ecstasy, during which a woman might seem to retreat to the deepest part of her being in search of paradises unimagined... I have even considered the possibility of—"

"No theories, please," I interrupted him brusquely, "just get to the point."

"I do beg your pardon," apologised Hilario, bowing his head like an animal instinctively recognising and acknowledging the superiority of a rival. "I tend to digress... I expect you would like to know how things went after that— how Lolita finally came to our domain, rural and desolate as it is. Naturally something went wrong: some ambiguity must have spluttered from my hasty pen (you know how treacherous words can be). Once more I gazed out of the window, and once more the garden was empty, and the road deserted apart from the occasional neighbour, or child on a bicycle; there was no one, certainly, who had come from the other side of the world... Then Emma went out for one of her lonely walks. She always followed the same route, taking in the hermitage, the ruined windmill, the pines along the river up to the top of the hill... She probably stopped there to look at our house in the distance before turning back. (She couldn't have imagined, of course, that while she was thus occupied I was endeavouring to betray her). That afternoon, I had resigned myself to yet another failure when I saw her reappear on the road, holding by the hand an adolescent clad only in a nightdress. I understood immediately: no village child would have ventured out dressed like that. I remember how I felt on seeing them open the gate – how can I explain it? – I was overtaken by an unfathomable excitement, a sort of ecstasy. It was as though I had momentarily brushed the hand of the Almighty. My delight only lasted a moment, while the pair were crossing the garden, but for those few star-struck seconds I imagined myself surrounded by literature's best-loved characters: Don Quixote, Juliet, Anna Karenina, the Karamazovs... They were all waiting there, in the front room of my house; tangible, moving, come to join me *in the land of the living...*"

FIVE

Hilario's eyes were wide open—worryingly, excessively so; his body, grubby jacket and all, appeared to be on the point of levitating. I feared for a moment his relapsing into one of his *ineffable* ecstasies. Fortunately, this did not occur, and I witnessed his return to the gloom of our provincial café. He strained to collect the scattered threads of his story.

"When… When they arrived in the house," he continued eventually, "I came down the stairs and discovered that the teenager seemed a lot more childlike than I had imagined. One could see nothing of Humbert's nymphet; her face contained none of that perverse allure that supposedly bewitched older men. As had been the case with Emma, she was so tired and confused that she could barely speak; she just looked at us with her large, heavy-lidded eyes. It seemed impossible to me that one could feel attracted to this worried little girl, who trembled to be looked at… Shaking with fear, she must have felt like a lost traveller on a foggy night. Over the next few days, I saw to it that she settled into our world after being so rudely torn from her own. Lolita's recovery proved nevertheless quicker than Emma's. She made an effort to communicate straight away because she knew a few words of French and some Spanish too. Like her predecessor, she didn't seem particularly interested in where she was; she only cared about her clothes and the contents of the fridge. I had to stock up on fizzy drinks, ice cream and sweets, as well as blouses, sandals and gaudy figure-hugging trousers. I won't hide from you, Altabella, that I was beginning to regret my foolishness; I missed my old life, solitary but peaceful. Sometimes I regretted rescuing Lolita. Emma didn't seem overly surprised by the teenager's presence—quite the opposite. She felt for her an immediate, boundless affection: an unhealthy tenderness. She dressed her, brushed her hair and satisfied her every whim. I often saw them laughing, whispering together, exchanging conspiratorial looks... Communicating in a strange mish-mash of French and English, they rapidly built a wall around themselves that I could not cross. I thought about abandoning them, disappearing, but I felt responsible—guilty, if you will. Looking for a way out of this desperate situation, I was tempted to reveal to them both their fate—not that such a revelation would have helped matters..."

Hilario's features had settled into a sorry, pathetic expression. It was surprising to see how easily he went from exaltation to defeat—or, rather, how perfectly he feigned both. Like an imbecile, I moved to touch his shoulder in reassurance; but I reined myself in, remembering once again that all this was nothing more than a joke, an absurd comedy, an amateurish fantasy.

"These past few weeks," continued Hilario, letting slip a deep sigh, "the situation has become unbearable. Emma has become – do you remember how Rodolphe described her – ever more *'tyrannical and interfering'*? I'm sure they are mocking me. I hear them laughing together at night (they've shared a room for more than a month) and when I'm there they communicate with words and gestures that mean nothing to me. The worst part now is that I'm afraid that the villagers will have the police investigate these mysterious visits. I've even considered…" Hilario leaned over the table-top and I recoiled, pressing myself against the back of my chair "… finishing them off. *Physically*, I mean; they are both immortal in the literary universe and will remain so. After all, no one would miss them, don't you think?"

I thought only that his horrid story was becoming ever more distasteful. I've always considered murders and murderers quite vulgar in fiction. I say that now: my visceral response was rather less measured.

Hilario reacted quickly, as though worried about frightening me with his morbid musings.

"I'm not serious, of course!" he said, faking another smile. "These stupid fantasies—I sometimes get carried away… Needless to say, the situation is both unbearable and compromising, and it worsens every day. Now my two guests want to meet the neighbours, establish a social life for themselves! Can you imagine what will happen if someone starts asking questions about their past?" Hilario chewed on his lip, sinking back into one of his sporadic silences.

The clock atop the neighbouring church struck eleven solemn, sonorous peals. Across the bar, a waiter with long, curly hair took advantage of the lull to devour a sandwich. That Hilario was capable of taking the joke this far filled me, despite myself, with both astonishment and admiration.

"Right," I said, breaking the silence. "Now, tell me the ending."

"The ending?"

"Yes, how does the story finish?"

Hilario fiddled with his coffee cup, pushing it around the saucer with a trembling little finger. "I'd like to know that myself," he replied.

"Come on, that's enough. You're obviously telling me a story—the plot of a novel or a plan for one. Admit it."

"I see! So, you haven't believed a word."

"You've tapped into the fantasy of every reader of Flaubert and Nabokov, I suspect; everyone who's ever fallen in love with Emma and Lolita dreams of such things."

"You think I've been pulling your leg?"

"Let's just say that you've used… quite an *original* method to interest me in your novel."

Hilario sighed dramatically.

"Now you know why I was so hesitant to approach you," he whispered, adopting an air of defeat. "I thought you might react like this."

His listlessness seemed to confirm my fears for his sanity, and I felt that I had to give him a few words of encouragement.

"I'm sure, Hilario, that after a few modifications, all this will make a most interesting short story."

While I was speaking, I had leaned forward slightly, placing my elbows on the table. Suddenly, Hilario did something that paralysed me: with a swift, cat-like movement, he grabbed my hands. His own were trembling.

"You must help me!" he whimpered imploringly.

I tried to free myself from his grasp without hurting his dignity, but his grip was more tenacious than I had expected in someone apparently so fragile. I felt ridiculous, trapped this way; I wondered what the shifty looking waiter, still eating his sandwich, must be thinking. Hilario didn't seem to notice my sudden distress.

"You must help me!" he repeated quietly, gazing intently into my eyes. The waiter must have thought that Hilario was making an unconventional declaration of love.

"Let me go first!" I fired back, my voice that of a child, thinking regretfully of my dandyish reputation, soon to be tarnished forever.

Quickly, silently, he released my hands; out of the corner of my eye I caught a glimpse of the waiter's curious expression. I felt another wave of pity for the poor fool opposite me and wondered how I could help him.

"I'd like you to speak to Emma," he said, a vague glimmer piercing his clouded gaze. "She's suffocating in that house. I've already told you that she wants to meet people, make friends… Well, Altabella—I want you to be her first friend. Perhaps her *confidant*, in time. And then, who knows, maybe more…"

I believe that the thing that made me lose my patience was not so much his absurd proposition, but rather the suggestiveness of that last phrase. I told him that his insistence was both monumentally boring and worrying, and that his refusal to give up the act was making me doubt his sanity.

Hilario listened stolidly to my outburst. His usual expression of horrified anticipation didn't change one whit. I gathered that my frankness had had no effect. Then came his reply—a conspiratorial:

"I'll prove it to you."

He rummaged in the large briefcase at his feet and pulled out a wrinkled bundle of cloth. Then, adopting the air of one who wishes to be secret and mysterious (making himself more grotesque and childish by the minute), he unfolded under my nose a small black cape, nondescript and worn with age. I examined it, puzzled. The waiter, who had stopped eating his sandwich, looked at us from the bar. I wondered what he must think of this new turn of events.

"You recognise this, don't you?" hissed Hilario.

"Recognise what?" I murmured, forcing myself to mimic his mysterious, conspiratorial tone.

"The tippet. The black tippet worn by Emma the morning she went to meet Leon!"

I vaguely remembered that Madame Bovary had donned for the occasion a silk dress, a hat and a short black cape, but only an imbecile would attempt to prove anything with such an item. Nevertheless, I took the piece of clothing from Hilario and looked at it closely for several seconds. It must have been at this moment that I realised that I was in the presence of a real literary character; not a character *from* a novel, of course, but someone capable of planting in me the seed of a couple of hundred pages of immortal fiction. I cursed myself for failing to grasp that I had had before me for the last two hours that self-same picturesque and singular character of whom all authors dream. I even regretted not having taken a furtive note or two under the table in order to capture his gestures, hesitations and unpredictable mannerisms. While I feigned interest in the ridiculous piece of cloth – doubtless inherited from one of his grandmothers – I began to consider the character. Which traits should I add or supress in order to make him realistic and acceptable to the reader? In my mind I wiped the scarecrowish expression from Hilario's face and declared him victim of a horrible childhood trauma, probably the root cause of the alienation which seemed to fuel his miserable existence… I daydreamed thus for eight or ten seconds; then, while the creative half of my brain continued to search for the formula which would transform this tortured individual into an unforgettable literary icon, the other half – that belonging to the sceptical intellectual, merciless critic, and sensible and respectable citizen – handed the tippet back to its owner and told him, eyebrows raised:

"This, Hilario, proves nothing at all."

My words must have annoyed him, for his face tensed slightly. By now, I was doing my utmost to observe his every movement in order to retain even the tiniest details. This new attentiveness permitted me to avoid his hands which, like claws, swiped at my own in a vain attempt to take hold of them.

"In that case, I beg you, please…" he replied carefully, as though overwhelmed, "… please come home with me."

SIX

When I look back now and reflect on the tortuous progress of his tale, it is not difficult for me to see the pains that Hilario had taken in his cunning preparations. Nevertheless, the dubious and subtle way in which he pushed me over the brink into the absurd, the inexplicable – into the arms of an unexpected destiny from which escape would prove impossible – will never cease to amaze me. It is clear to me now that his extravagant surveillance campaign and his ridiculous appeal for help were both part of a perfidious plan whose only objective was to encourage me to follow him home. The reader should know, however, that it was not this complicated strategy that caught me in the end. I believed not a word of his ramblings. If I fell into the trap, it was certainly not because the two heroines *brought back to life* had aroused my curiosity. The only thing that made me accept Hilario's pressing invitation was my desire to write a book about *him*. It was to be the masterpiece that would fling open for me the narrow doorway of literary immortality: the extraordinary story of an amateur writer forever scarred by literature's most famous works. Far from bothering me, the parallel that would be drawn with Quixote, that unforgettable *hidalgo* driven mad by tales of chivalry, seemed to indicate that my work was heading in a most promising direction…

That night, while I forced myself, like a punctilious vampire, to ingest every detail of Hilario's incredible face, thinning hair and threadbare jacket, I was tormented by the idea that at any moment he could stand up and disappear forever over the horizon, leaving me alone with my unfinished masterpiece. That was why, when he repeated his emotional invitation a few minutes later, I decided to follow him. I wanted to see how far his ramblings would lead. At first, I feigned reasonable reluctance:

"Perhaps it would be better to do it another day. I haven't eaten, and—"

"Don't worry about dinner," replied Hilario, "we'll have a bite at mine. I have an interesting wine I'd like you to taste."

"It's a tad late for visitors, don't you think?"

"No need for formalities! Emma will be delighted to meet you. I've told her so much about you! I even told her that we were meeting in town today. She'll be so disappointed if you don't come."

I argued a little, without conviction, and when at last I accepted his invitation, I felt a prickle of anxiety which quickly swelled into a profound sense of anguish. Hilario, conversely, perked up considerably; he stood up and strode to the bar. I hurried after him and, under the watchful eye of the sideburn-sporting barman, we argued for a moment over who should pay the bill. (A ploy: suddenly apprehensive, I made a scene in order to have the man as a witness.) *Given that I am coming to yours*, I said loudly to Hilario, *it's only right that I pay for the drinks…*

Adopting a disarmingly comic air, he accepted, and as the barman handed me my change, I asked my gracious host if his village was far away. I think he detected my ruse immediately, because he answered with a laconic *we'll be there soon.*

When we left the café, the heat of that August night seemed heavier and more all-enveloping than ever; while we walked towards Hilario's car, I began sweating excessively. I remember looking around for a familiar face, someone whom I could tell about my foolhardy plan. But at that late hour, the few acquaintances I still had in the city were all probably busy watching one of those erotic films broadcast on German television. We finally stopped in front of a large car which was every bit as battered- looking as its driver. Once installed within, Hilario lifted the large chain from the steering wheel and started the worn old engine, which roared ferociously as soon as the vehicle started moving. I shook with trepidation as we drove through the streets; for the first few minutes, I cherished the hope that a part of the engine would drop onto the road out of the city centre. It was not to be, and I contemplated – without knowing, of course, that I was doing so for the last time – the black hill cutting through the red-brick buildings of the city, the ghostly curved walls of the service station two kilometres from the northern bypass.

We soon left the main road for another, full of potholes and bumps which made the car's entrails rumble. I remember my chauffeur turning to look at me and that at that precise moment I once more had the alarming feeling that I was in the company of a total stranger. I reflected on the possible outcomes of our trip. The best-case scenario had Hilario, breathless and confused, searching through every room in his house before telling me that the two spectres had inexplicably disappeared. He would finish by admitting that it had all been a ruse to persuade me to read one of his impossible manuscripts. (This scene led to another, where I saw myself bestowing sage advice to the poor deluded amateur over one of those smoked hams abundant in country homes.) The second possibility was much more worrying: I envisaged the car braking before a hospital and the hero of my novel disappearing inside with a maniacal laugh, leaving me alone in the darkness. The image of Emma Bovary and Lolita Haze opening the front door to us also crossed my mind, only to be immediately dismissed by that incorruptible mental censor tasked with making sense from fantasy.

All the while, the car continued to climb steep sloping hills, its headlights illuminating impenetrable stretches of countryside as we cut through silent villages. Sometimes, like silent harbingers of doom, the ruins of a hermitage or the sharp crest of a hill surged out of the darkness. After fifteen or twenty kilometres, the notion of introducing this man into one of my books tempted me far less than it had in the café; my regard had changed from that of a novelist eager to capture every detail of his personality to that of a lost traveller, placatory victim, or unhappy spectator coerced onstage by a deranged magician.

We had been driving for about half an hour when Hilario announced that we had arrived. A few more houses, weakly-lit and barely discernible in the night; then a bridge over an inky black stream. Finally, the car stopped before a solitary two-storey building.

It is probable that, set against the splendour of a Castilian sunset, the house would have been in no way frightening. It is also likely that, during the day, the stone walls would have taken on the same ashen grey colour as any noble country dwelling, that the chimneys and lintels would have held nothing more than tiles and television aerials. At that time of night, however, the building brought to mind a livid face crowned with thorns. That was how it seemed to me as I peered through the car's window. Hilario killed the engine and plunged us into the desolate, motionless silence of that dreary place.

No lights were burning in the front windows but, from the back of the house, a bluish light filtered through the darkness. Hilario lost a few seconds in reattaching the chain to the steering wheel (as if a car like his would have interested anyone in that part of the country!), then turned to me. Once more I beheld that changeable face, those unknowable features.

"Please don't tell Emma of her tragic end," he murmured.

That was, I believe, the first time I thought that this man's madness might prove dangerous.

Contrary to expectations, the garden gate barely creaked when we opened it, but the house was no less fearsome for that. Walking up the gravel path, I noticed a few trees on my right; the stonework around the front door, still warm from its day in the sun, strengthened my first impression of the building as a living organism. That memory is now mixed with that of the stifling sensation that came over me as I crossed the threshold, probably due to both the rarefied atmosphere and the sombre striped pattern of the living-room wallpaper, giving the place an oppressive, antiquated air. Hilario invited me to sit in one of the armchairs, but I felt so out of sorts in that room that I went straight to the window. Outside, nothing but a hostile blanket of darkness: the metallic outline of the car had been swallowed by the night and only the silhouette of a wood – far off on the other side of the valley, no doubt – stood out against the horizon. I thought it best to give my gracious host the opportunity to admit that the whole story had merely been a pretext for bringing me there.

"I think you can come clean, Hilario," I said, gazing up at the trembling outline of the Great Bear. "Now I'm here, you might as well show me your manuscript."

Obtaining no reply, I turned round and saw that the hero of my third novel had disappeared. I went to the room's only exit: an opening hidden by a pair of heavy green curtains. Behind these lay a corridor and gloomy staircase which let in a draught of cool air. A faint chopping sound came from upstairs and (no doubt due to my hunger) I suddenly thought of Hilario carving slices of ham. I stepped back into the small living room, where every item of furniture – the enormous mahogany bookcase, dour piano pushed against the wall, sofa and armchairs covered in dark velvet upholstery – only reinforced my feeling of suffocation. On the striped wallpaper hung a number of hunting scenes of dogs, horses, red riding jackets and tiny foxes hiding in the bushes, and a few edifying engravings. I went to the bookcase. Nothing teaches one more about a man's soul than the books he would have liked to have read. There I found, stacked in a kind of endearing disorder, a few worthy classics; but these were swamped by a much larger quantity of esoteric guides and gardening manuals. Behind two glazed doors, the lower shelves held eight or ten impeccably-ranked volumes, the tidiness of which contrasted sharply with the disorder above. All were bound in leather, their spines inscribed with elegant gold letters. I had to crouch down to make out the titles. The frame of the door almost entirely hid the first volume, but *Romeo and Juliet* was legible on the second. Underneath this were printed two names: W. Shakespeare and H. Campillo. Propelled by curiosity, I continued, scoffing, to read the titles: *Macbeth* and *Othello*, by the same authors – I imagined Desdemona's last-minute escape from her husband's demented clutches – and a *Don Quixote* displaying, alongside the sacred name of Cervantes, that of his deranged defiler. *The Red and the Black* was also the work of Stendhal-Campillo. That man had decided to take on all the heroes of world literature. As the volumes were arranged in chronological order, I noticed, scanning from left to right, that the great authors disappeared altogether as the centuries dragged on, leaving only the name of their pig-headed 'collaborator'. I would have liked to have taken a proper look at such a grotesque collection of horrors, but alas—the glass doors were locked.

When I stood up (biting my lip to keep from laughing), I noticed on one of the shelves, between a manual on *Maintaining your Classic Car* and the complete works of the Marquis de Sade, a copy of my own first novel. I couldn't resist the delicious temptation to browse through it once more and, in so doing, I discovered to my surprise and horror that the pages were full of corrections and insulting comments. Someone had seen fit to mark chapter five as *plagiarism*, twelve times; and the same hand had written – this time in capital letters – *IMBECILE!* in the margin of a sublime paragraph that had taken me four days to complete. Dumbfounded, I leafed through the rest of the novel, searching for further traces of the enraged reader. Eight or ten hideous caricatures occupied the blank inside covers. I thought I recognised myself in one of them, then finally understood that they were all, to varying degrees of likeness, my own portrait. I put the novel back in its place and staggered to one of the armchairs, afraid of finding a copy of my second novel elsewhere in the shelves. This man hated me, I had no doubt, and his incomprehensible invitation was no more than a trap to entice me to my death…

As I gave myself over to these distressing reflections, I heard someone behind me:

"Sorry for the wait."

It was the voice of that hypocritical vermin. I leapt up and saw on his face an innocent smile. How I would have loved to have knocked him down there and then! But I had to compose myself, for standing beside him was a small, pale-faced woman. She was pretty and dressed quite strangely. It was as though she had lost all her possessions in a shipwreck and someone had loaned her the outdated blouse, long skirt and old-fashioned shoes that she was wearing. The young woman held out her hand and I briefly squeezed her delicate fingers. Her hand was strangely cool, and pulled back quickly from my touch, as though afraid of imprisonment within.

"*Hilaguio* has told me about you," she said. Her tone was affectionate or trying to be so. "I've seen your photograph in the newspapers. I'm afraid I don't understand Spanish. But you know my language, *n'est-ce pas?*"

While she was speaking, Hilario threw me a veiled glance, hoping perhaps that this would establish between us a certain complicity. I ignored him. For it was now that I began to suspect myself of being the victim of a stupid joke. There must have been a tape recorder hidden somewhere; they would play back my stupid replies and laugh themselves silly, I thought.

"I've heard of you too, *madame*," I answered mockingly.

She burst into a smile and sat down on the sagging, fraying sofa. During the silence that followed, I observed her black hair pinned up at the sides, her large dark eyes crowned with thick brows. Her features could well have been those of Emma Bovary, there was little doubt; but her apparent coldness did not seem to correspond with the character. Flaubert's heroine would probably have looked at me, young and handsome as I was, with a little more interest.[3] Hilario had failed to mention her name when introducing us; he was, perhaps, at last ashamed of the hoax that they had doubtless spent days preparing. He now stood close to me, as though wanting to hang on to my every word, but I kept my lips sealed. After three or four questions, I would easily unravel this grotesque prank, for I knew Flaubert's novel far better than either of them...

---

[3] Once more we are confronted with Germán Altabella's incorrigible (and invented) *Don-Juan*ism. The reader should note that he was not as *young* as implied at the time of these events. (Note: Mario Pallochi)

When the silence became more pressing, like a gelatinous glue which would entrap us forever, I decided to seize the initiative:

"Do you like our region?" I asked the young woman in Spanish, hoping to catch her unawares.

"*Pardon?*" she replied, looking up at me. The darkness of her eyes, contrasting with the pallor of her face, imbued her with melancholy.

"I wanted to know if you liked our *région*," I repeated in French. From that point onwards, our conversation continued in that language, which she spoke exquisitely (Hilario, on the other hand, expressed himself haphazardly, with little regard for syntax).

"If you must know," she said, with a sideways scowl at her host, "I hate the countryside with all my heart."

Hilario, to whom these words seemed to be addressed, scratched his neck several times, and in a few monosyllables of schoolboy French declared that he was going to make us something to eat. The young woman's expression seemed to soften a little when he left the room. I even thought that she was going to tell me something to put an end to the whole tasteless joke, but she only added: "...if you'll excuse my saying so."

"There's no need to apologise. We should always tell the truth, *n'est-ce pas?*"

"Perhaps," she replied. She kept her legs pressed tightly together, as though ashamed that I could see her sturdy white calves.

"I don't like the countryside either," I continued, allowing myself a frank confession. "Fortunately, you don't live very far from the city. I suppose Hilario drives you there often enough."

"He did… at the beginning," she said. "I remember that everyone seemed to be in a rush…" Amused, she looked at me for a moment and shook her head. "Do you not find it strange to see people roaring through the streets like madmen in those noisy automobiles?"

"But it's just a backwater! What would you say of Madrid or Paris? You've visited Paris, I'm sure…" I added blandly, hoping again to trap her.

"No," she answered with a gentle sigh. "But I've dreamt of going so often!"

There was a calculated naivety in her tone; clearly she was much slyer than I had imagined. But I still could not understand why she had agreed to play a part in these stupid theatrics.

"Ask your husband to take you there—"

"—*Hilaguio* is not my husband!" she exclaimed, blushing with surprising intensity. "Anyway, I don't think that he would want to."

"Why don't we talk about him?" I asked, staring impertinently into her eyes.

"I would rather not."

I was on the point of telling her what I thought of that imbecile when we heard laughter from the floor above. Her face tensed visibly. Her spirit, on the other hand, seemed to have found refuge elsewhere—it was hiding somewhere far from that slender, tangible, unmysterious body before me. The role must have been so taxing for her.

"I would like to know what made you decide to come here." She raised her voice a little, perhaps to cover the laughter that continued to echo through the ceiling.

"Hilario said that you'd like to meet me."

"Ah, that..."

"Wasn't it true?"

"He said that you probably knew me better than I knew myself," replied the young woman, furtively trying to adjust her skirt.

Now it was her turn to set me a trap. She must have been enjoying herself behind that glacial mask.

"I don't think I know any more about you than he's told me himself," I replied hesitantly, weighing my every word.

The high, childish laughter pealed through the house again and I began to wonder if there could be a television camera somewhere, capturing my perplexity for the benefit of some unknown audience. I was becoming annoyed. If they wanted to laugh, why not let me in on the joke? I stood up, ready to put an end to the farce.

"Doesn't it strike you as a little *imprudent* of Hilario to leave me alone with... such an attractive woman?" I murmured, advancing towards her with the sneer of a horror-film villain.

"I run no risk with you, I'm sure."

"What if I told you differently?"

"I would think you were teasing me."

"Teasing…?" I repeated, sitting down beside her. "But you have no idea of how many times I've imagined this encounter. How many times I've dreamed of stroking your hair, kissing your lips, then losing myself in your *irresistible sensuality*!" I concluded, my voice that of an actor in the worst kind of romantic melodrama.

I saw her tense. Her expression remained the same, as if wishing to show no fear. She must have been starting to weigh up the risks of this little charade.

"Are you not worried about Hilario coming in?" she asked me.

"The only thing that worries me is not getting another chance to tell you how I feel," I replied, taking her hand. A rapid tremor ran through her whole body.

"You are an impetuous man," she said, her eyes wide and fixed on mine.

We were now both reciting the lines of some old comedy, perhaps a vaudeville scene. The thought encouraged me to kiss her delicate fingers and, in so doing, I noticed seeping from her skin a plant-like odour, a strange smell of paper pulp. The young woman blushed once more but did not move.

"Your manners surprise me somewhat," she said coldly, as though to demonstrate that my kiss had touched not a single fibre of her sensibility.

"I am merely tormented by the thought that you could evaporate at any moment in the heat of this room and disappear forever," I whispered (holding back my laughter) in her delicious ear, barely visible beneath the inky waves of her hair.

She inhaled deeply, as though preparing to jump from a diving board. By now, I was ready to smash through the limits of decency in order to bring the masquerade to a swift conclusion. She, on her side, seemed unwilling to admit defeat. She had probably been instructed to carry things through to the bitter end.

"I believe that someone is coming," she said, nodding at the door.

"That old trick!" I exclaimed, my tone falsely jovial. "But this time you won't fool anyone."

"You mock me!" she said, looking me straight in the eye, and for the first time I was seized by a sudden frisson of lust. (I must confess that, upon seeing the candour of those deep-black pupils, I almost gave the game away; but it was my first acting role, and I couldn't allow her to steal the limelight.)

"You don't know how many millions of readers dream of having you close to them, *Emma*; how many dream of gazing upon you, of caressing you, of declaring their love…" I began with all the ardour of a provincial Don Juan. And while I showered her with those flowery compliments, full of specious passion, I planted a slow kiss on her cheek, breathing in the coolness that rose from her skin and forgetting that this unknown woman could be, *at the very worst*, the wife of Hilario Campillo. I noticed rapidly that, without giving up completely, she was forgetting her role and was ceding to my shameless assault. It was then (too late for me to believe that her words were sincere) that she murmured, sighing with pleasure:

"I will scream."

Secure in the knowledge that she would do nothing of the sort, I tried to change my inveigling approach into an embrace worthy of the volcanic ardour of Flaubert's heroine. I heard her groan softly once or twice, biting her lip; but immediately afterwards, as though subject to a shifting and contradictory impulse, she disengaged herself from my grasp and stood up, leaving me in the concupiscent attitude of a rampant lion. Her delicate ears, smaller but much more sensitive than my own, had detected a familiar footstep on the other side of the curtain.

SEVEN

Hilario caught me on the sofa, hair rumpled, and shirt soaked in sweat. He was carrying a tray and threw me one of those exasperating glances, to which I was already becoming accustomed, before opening his mouth:

"I hope you like ham," he said, placing before me a plate piled with fleshy pink slices. Much like an astronomer might attest to the existence of a new planet without ever putting his eye to a telescope, I had *sensed* its presence in the house. Hilario opened a small cupboard and took out a good bottle of Rioja. The young woman had approached the window and gazed through it now with stupefying indifference, as though our host were nothing more than one of those shadowy waiters whose face we forget as soon as the restaurant door closes behind us.

While the master of the house uncorked the bottle, I wondered how far the pair of them would be willing to go. I know that I could have asked him to drive me back to the city but, at that moment in time, I had two good reasons to stay. The first one was the porcelain plate on the table; the second, the lascivious encounter that had just taken place and which seemed to hold the promise of greater things to come.

Perching carefully on the edge of one of the armchairs, Hilario poured me a glass. The three of us were now positioned in an imaginary isosceles triangle, with Emma's dark and motionless silhouette forming the most distant point.

"*Nothing to drink, Emma?*" asked our host in broken French.

She shook her head and I feared that she might be considering putting an end to the farce (and, at the same time, to my lustful hopes).

"Sit with us, at least!" Hilario continued, in a tone of forced amiability.

This time, the young woman didn't even bother to respond.

The plate of ham shone up at me, hot and tempting; and since I could do nothing as victim of the strange hoax, I decided to behave as a death-row prisoner who, faced with the electric chair, astonishes his executioners with a stupefying show of appetite.

No one spoke as I lifted the first few slices to my lips, and the scene soon resembled one of those silent family conferences with someone preparing to make a dramatic announcement along the lines of "we're ruined", or "I'm divorcing that bitch".

"Did you know that Emma loves moonlit walks?" said Hilario, suddenly.

That must have been an addition to the plot, for I did not remember Flaubert's heroine ever taking any such walk, unless to meet a lover.

"She sometimes stays out for hours. Then she comes in numb and shivering with cold," he continued, his tone almost sinister. "I don't understand her love of the dark."

"Then again, who really understands a woman's heart?" I replied jovially, lifting to my lips another huge mouthful of ham.

"Do you not love to gaze upon the stars?" Emma addressed me from her spot by the window.

"There aren't stars in the city anymore!" I joked. "These days we light up the streets because we're afraid to face the terrible immensity of the universe."

She smiled incredulously, and Hilario took advantage of the lull to refill my glass. I suddenly thought that if there had been poison in the bottle, I was already beyond help.

"In a way, the night brings us face to face with the... *mysteries* of existence and the... *fragility* of our own lives," observed Hilario hesitantly in his inaccurate French.

"That's why it's better to sleep, to dream, to seek refuge in the arms of women we love!" I replied, the alcohol rousing the dormant poet within me.

"We can also lose ourselves in the heavens, like a comet or a cloud of dust," ventured the supposed wife of Charles Bovary, doubtless spurred on by my lyrical nonsense.

"Nevertheless, the only sensible, reasonable thing to do is not to lose ourselves or disappear, but rather to *observe*, to *question*, to *understand*," declared Hilario, who now came across, bizarrely, as the most rational member of our party.

"Why do men have this idiotic desire to explain everything?" cried Emma suddenly, throwing Hilario a look of utter disdain.

"*Et, en plus, quand le mystère est trop grand...!*" I said, citing an old French proverb which does not merit translation.

Hilario shook his head.

"One day, humanity will have shed light on every mystery," he said gravely.

This was all becoming rather tedious. We looked like three conspirators who had lost the plot. I shuddered to think of spending the rest of the night drinking wine and exchanging platitudes. A cunning idea came to me:

"May I ask you a question, Emma?" I said, making my voice as innocent as possible.

From the furthest point of the isosceles, the young woman threw me a serious, solemn look.

"Would you like to play us a tune on the piano?" I continued, turning towards the austere instrument, which seemed to observe us from its corner of the room (Flaubert's supposed heroine would *have to* know how to play).

"It's just an old, out-of-tune Gaveau..." Hilario began, shifting uncomfortably in his chair.

"I love music," I insisted, privately rejoicing to see them so embarrassed, "especially from an old out-of-tune Gaveau."

"I have not played for over one hundred years," said Emma calmly, displaying admirable presence of mind.

"But pianos die if no one plays them!" I joked.

"Emma must be afraid of disappointing you," suggested Hilario, who had fallen prey to a dreadful tic in his left shoulder, which was twitching with alarming frequency.

"I promise... to practise a little before your next visit," said Emma.

I adopted a somewhat dramatic tone: "There might not be another visit," I said, helping myself to more ham.

Emma looked worried: "You might not come back?"

"That depends on you," I replied, trying unsuccessfully to catch her eye.

She hesitated, then slowly crossed the room, as though doubting the solidity of the floor. She seemed taller to me than she had at first; the curve of her hip was even more alluring. An old clock, running slow, ponderously chimed the twelve strokes of midnight. The young woman sat at the piano and waited for the noise (so strange and metallic and urgent!) to stop, then launched into a graceful, romantic leitmotif. I could only accept defeat. Still, she seemed to play with more doggedness than passion, as if her only goal were to navigate the piece without making a mistake. Again, I glimpsed the poor twitching fool from the corner of my eye and wondered at his strange agitation. It could not have come from any lack of musical talent on the part of his heroine, as her skill was beyond question; every detail had been carefully prepared. Then I remembered the curious incident of which he had told me in the café: the visit of that piano-tuner who, seduced by the young *revenante*, had left without finishing his work. Another tall tale, of course: the piano seemed perfectly tuned. Hilario must have been worrying about that. But what did one more fib matter? Like a stack of Russian dolls, Hilario's story was built of lie upon lie, sprinkled with incongruities; the whole thing apparently dreamt up by the seething imagination of a madman. Why had he spun me a tale that only added to the proverbial promiscuity of the woman's character? It was as though Hilario had wished to present her as even more wanton and accessible than in the novel—as though he had wanted to make me think that I could easily have her, just by desiring her... Indeed! If my suspicions were justified, I could only conclude that Hilario had brought me to his home *in order to seduce this woman*! I know that the idea was rather troubling, rather perverse; however, while my supposed prey was clumsily attacking a famous Bach *étude*, I began to draw together a number of hypotheses, all of which led to the same conclusion. Firstly, the householder wanted revenge (not without reason, I admitted), and after having encouraged me – more or less subtly – to seduce his wife, he was planning on bursting in at the last moment and taking my life with a well-aimed bullet to the heart. As this deed would surely cost him many years in prison, we would have to see if his hatred and desire to wipe me out were strong enough to carry him through his sentence.

The second hypothesis, less distressing, saw Hilario Campillo as the victim and the instigator this woman who, eye for an eye, hoped to avenge her husband's infidelities with a short-lived but passionate affair with a local celebrity. I couldn't begin to grasp why the wife of my host had disguised herself as Flaubert's heroine! But I remember thinking – helped, no doubt, by the excellent Rioja – that this theory was the most plausible, given both the young woman's visible resentment of Hilario and my conviction that one man could never entreat another to make love to his wife.

The idea of becoming thus embroiled in a sensual encounter made me look with new eyes upon the curve of her breasts, standing out pert and assertive against the drab black of the piano.

"To your taste?" Hilario whispered in my ear, his voice trembling. I understood that he was speaking not of the melodies being tapped out with childlike concentration, but of the young woman he was dangling before me with such aplomb.

I acquiesced with a wry smile, an expression that I hoped would convey that, having caught on to the trick, hare-brained as it was, I was willing to play the lewd (but fascinating) role assigned to me. Still twitching, Hilario grinned back, and I couldn't help feeling a rush of compassion for the poor libertine who had been forced to set up his own punishment. I was wondering at what moment he would finally decide to quit the room, leaving us two alone, when I spotted, near the doorway leading onto the corridor, a pale adolescent clad in a large shirt and denim jeans rolled up to her knees. She must have been twelve or thirteen years old, but dark shadows were already forming beneath her pale grey eyes, which observed me with ironic curiosity. Raising an ink- or varnish-streaked finger to her lips, the newcomer implored me not to reveal her presence, then turned to look at our indefatigable pianist, who continued to play out her repertoire of *pièces faciles*. The girl's unexpected appearance made the endless concert slightly more interesting; I remember observing her bare feet, her toenails daubed with cherry-red varnish and her long hair, imitating the pianist's own, pulled up into a graceful chignon.

When this delicious creature looked at me again, above Hilario's thinning scalp, I thought I could read in her eyes a subtle glimmer of perversity—but that may have been the reflection of my own lascivious adult gaze. I amused myself by comparing her little freckled nose with Hilario's own long beak, then with the seductive profile of the pianist, without finding any resemblance between them. (She could have been adopted, I mused.) At the same time, the young girl was trying out a whole range of ridiculous poses in an attempt to catch my avid eye. There was no need to raise her arms to fiddle with her topknot, nor to stand with her hands on her hips like a water-carrier, nor tangle her long legs in one of the green curtains in front of the doorway. The latter proved her downfall; the wooden curtain rings emitted a xylophonic clacking noise, which made the man of the house turn around. I noticed him flushing intensely as though, finding himself in the middle of the street, he had suddenly realised that he wasn't wearing any trousers.

"Upstairs! Now!" he ordered, his voice much calmer than his words suggested.

The pianist was fighting her way through a tedious crescendo and barely seemed to notice the row going on behind her.

"I don't want to go upstairs," whispered the child in an American accent.

Hilario inhaled deeply and sank back into his cavernous seat. As might have been expected, this had no effect on the newcomer, who remained near the door with one of her adorable little feet planted against the wall. Brow furrowed in an affected sulk, her jaws dug a wad of chewing-gum from its resting place behind her damp, bright teeth, and her plump lips stretched to blow the fascinated visitor an ephemeral bubble which burst amidst the tumultuous piano chords. And after having waggled another dirty finger in my direction – signalling to me, as fellow conspirator, to hold my peace – she stalked forward like a tiger cub towards the armchair that had swallowed the householder. The latter must have anticipated her silent assault because he was perched expectantly, the rigidity of his body only troubled by the recurrent twitching of his left shoulder. The girl's hands ran over the velvet backrest, feeling for a Hilario Campillo paralysed with fear, and I thought about how much I would have enjoyed falling prey to those two pink serpents now tormenting their terrified victim; pinching him here, tickling him there, then gliding inside his threadbare jacket. The caresses seemed somewhat less than innocent. Silent and tenacious, they compelled the victim to contort himself grotesquely, to cross his arms, his small body listing from side to side. I saw that Hilario's face remained as flushed as it had been upon the little demon's arrival, and that his eyes avoided my own. He fixed his gaze upon the nape of the pianist's neck—she was hammering away at the supposed crowning glory of her recital. (One might have said that in the depths of her soul, mysterious as it was, she hated that horrible instrument.) By craning over one of the arms of my chair, I was still able to glimpse the intruder's provocative little nose, and her eyes, which were too wise and too jaded for her tender years. I was beginning to wonder how long the furtive struggle would last, when the more audacious of the serpents slipped to the lower part of the armchair and *bit* the occupant just above the ankle. This gesture, loaded with biblical symbolism, drew a stifled cry from the victim, which made our zealous performer turn her head. It took her two or three seconds to establish the cause of the disruption, then four or five more to interrupt her piece. She stood up with unusual violence. After the tedious concert, the silence which bore down on the living room was like a refreshing rain shower after a hot, airless afternoon.

For several minutes, none of us moved, as though paralysed by the sudden change. Then the young woman went to the window with a fearful, hesitant step and stood before the glass, contemplating the crescent moon or the little upland wood, sharply visible on the other side of the stream. Perhaps she was waiting for the master of the house to leave in order to bring her tortuous vengeance to its conclusion. Hilario did precisely that, albeit with some difficulty—our young visitor had set herself against the back of the chair and was refusing to leave. He had to seize her by the arm and drag her to the door; as she was being removed, the girl gazed at me with consuming intensity and blew me one last bubble, which popped silently against the delicate softness of her lips.

My penultimate memory of Hilario Campillo has him leaving the room, his expression asinine, his socks rolling down around his ankles and his old jacket rumpled. Upon reaching the door, he turned towards me and began to stammer, indicating his delectable prisoner:

"It's... it's..."

I smiled like a fellow conspirator. "*Lolita*, of course!"

EIGHT

By now, I believed both that I knew the role of each actor in this outlandish family farce and that I could anticipate their movements. I realised that we had begun the third act, during which, if my second hypothesis were correct, my host's wife, in the guise of Flaubert's heroine, would abandon herself to my lustful machinations. Her behaviour was, of course, the stuff of fantasy; but I imagined that the young woman's personality change had been intended to alleviate her natural modesty and understandable distress at the situation. I must admit that when Hilario left us alone, I too felt anxious: my most recent love affair had taken place five years previously, during one of those organised tours favoured by impossible aged spinsters and unapproachable beauties, and my sporadic relationship with one of the former had left a bitter taste in my mouth. But of course, that frigid old maid held not a candle to the charming little woman now standing by the window, gazing out at the veiled obscurity of the garden…

Suppose that she was to avenge herself there, on that fraying sofa… I had a flash of myself half-naked; my body, shaken by wild spasms, intertwined with her milk-white frame. Then – uncanny superposition – the ghostly figure of Hilario burst into my dream, toting a gun, ready to disprove my hypothesis. Although I managed to wipe the image from my mind immediately, I still wondered if, when the time came, my fear of such a scene would not jam the natural mechanisms of my lust.

"Sometimes," she said suddenly without turning, "I dream of being carried to the gallop of four horses towards a new land and, from a mountaintop there, of glimpsing some splendid city with domes, and bridges, and ships, forests of citron trees, and cathedrals of white marble…"

It was, as the reader has surely recognised, a paragraph from *Madame Bovary*. She must have known whole pages by heart.

"Here too we have forests, bridges, beautiful cathedrals…" I suggested, spurred by a sudden sense of patriotism.

"I have always found your famous gothic cathedral somewhat sinister," she said with a cold smile.

It was no moment for contradictions. I approached and began to caress her back, as one might stroke a recalcitrant horse before attempting to fix its saddle. The young woman spun around and clung to me clumsily, convulsively.

"Save me!" she begged. "Save me from this abominable place!"

I wondered if that was another line from the novel, but I couldn't place it in any chapter.

"For pity's sake, take me with you," she exclaimed, burying her face between my shirt buttons.

The idea of finally bringing her risky vengeance to fruition must have incited this strange reaction. She had probably never been unfaithful to her imbecile of a husband. I tried to calm her by holding her to my chest. Her hair exuded that same heavy, organic odour of paper pulp. I pressed my burning face against her pale, cold cheeks; then I slipped a hand between her body and my own, placing it adroitly on her breast. She recoiled immediately, suddenly fierce.

"What do you think you are doing? I want your help. I only want you to take me away from this horrible mansion," she said tragi-comically, backing away towards the wall, where she remained as though pasted to the sombre striped paper.

She exaggerated: Hilario's 'mansion' was nothing more than a family house. She too must have been a little ill in the head. Perhaps they were all mad and amused themselves every so often by staging this same spooky melodrama.

"I thought that you and I…" I said stupidly, moving towards her.

I saw her step back, spreading her hands against the wall like an enormous black-eyed spider.

"Don't come any closer or I will scream," she warned, her voice panicked and tearful.

"Who are you?" I asked, halting my impetuous advance.

"You know who I am."

"You don't think that I swallowed any of Hilario's nonsense?"

"What nonsense?"

"He insists that you're a character from a novel."

"Of course, I am. We all are, deep down."

"Very astute!" I said with a wan, forced smile.

This meandering conversation irritated me. I decided that it was time to unmask the players of this comedy.

"I don't suppose you would be embarrassed if I asked you a few questions…" I started as delicately as possible.

"What sort of question?"

"I only want some details about your life."

"I thought you knew about my life better than I did."

"I want to check that you know about it too."

"My memory is poor, but if there's no other way…" she said, moving closer to the window, once again affording me a glimpse of her delicious, melancholy profile.

Like the host of some tedious television game-show, I started to reel off questions: the origins of the doctor who preceded Charles Bovary in Yonville; her two subscription magazines; her maiden name; the subject of the small pencil sketch which hung in her father's house…[4] She was silent for a long time before answering, as though she had great difficulty in remembering. But she was much cleverer than her hesitancy at first implied. At the end, she turned to me with a triumphant smile:

"Do you believe me now?"

"I believe you know the novel by heart. You must have studied it for a long time… But there must be hundreds of Flaubert scholars in the world."

"You unbelieving, obstinate man!" she exploded, furious, and started to pace the living room.

"But I admire *your* obstinacy—I don't understand how you've taken the joke so far. I know, of course, what you're trying to hide from me."

"I am hiding nothing. I just want to leave this place."

"Don't lie to me. You're Hilario's wife and you've dreamt up this silly little game together. He's been watching my comings and goings in town for weeks."

"I do not know where *Hilaguio* goes when he leaves the house. And I am certainly not married to him."

"Let's say that you're… lovers, then."

"Do you not think it impertinent to suggest such things to a lady?" she retorted, biting her lip as she turned away from me.

"But no one cares about that type of thing these days!"

---

[4] Flaubert devotees can test their knowledge by answering the above questions. (Note: Mario Pallochi)

"Perhaps that's because people these days respect nothing."

"Remember," I said, accepting for a tiny fraction of a second the infinitesimal possibility that she might really be Emma Bovary, "– remember that you, too, once lacked respect for a certain doctor…"

I saw her turn around again, swept up in theatrical indignation:

"You odious man! Like Rodolphe! Like *Hilaguio* Campillo! Like all men!" she exclaimed, stifling a sob.

"And yet, when we were alone just now, you didn't seem repulsed by my touch."

"I feared that you would leave. I needed your help; you are the first man to come here in such a long time."

I was looking at her with growing prurient admiration, piqued not by the inflexions of her voice or her quick-witted answers, but above all by her curious see-sawing between distress and ferocity, posturing and lassitude.

"I must admit that you play the part magnificently," I said, raising my glass to her in a toast.

"You are a cynic, señor Altabella," she answered, wiping her tears with a small handkerchief.

"Perhaps we could say the same of you."

"Indeed?" she asked, raising her eyes to meet my own. The tears swimming therein conferred (to use a cliché) a sort of sombre magnetism.

"I suspect that you're using me in order to avenge your… *lover's* infidelity."

"I've never heard anything so ridiculous!" she retorted, blowing her nose.

"Come now. Why not admit that Hilario's been unfaithful?"

"Of course, I admit it. He spends his days chasing after that brat, that little hussy!"

"What? His own daughter?"

"She isn't his daughter! She just *arrived* in this house like an abandoned child, with her insupportable vulgarity and then he…" The sentence hung in the air, unfinished, as more laughter rang down from the floor above: "—just listen to them, playing their obscene games!"

"You shouldn't be so hard on the girl," I said, my tone somewhere between teasing and cruelty. "She's only a character in a novel."

"You mock me still!" the young woman exclaimed, fixing me with a stare. "You think yourself more consistent than us, more solid than us, Altabella. Let me tell you how wrong you are. You are *vague, imprecise*. No two readers have the same image of you—not of your face, nor of your voice…"

"I don't know which *readers* you're talking about," I interrupted, feeling strangely and suddenly offended at seeing myself again compared to a 'character in a novel'.

"But of course, you do!" she snapped. "As for the readers, I am sure that they think *themselves* much more real, much more consistent than *us*. But, you see, *we* are immortal."

"I'm sorry I can't aspire to this comforting *immortality* of which you speak. I feel terribly limited, terribly ephemeral—" I stood up decisively, ready to prove to this obstinate woman the reality of my existence. "I'm going to show you that I'm not a character from a novel. No character from a novel could create others, living in other books, as I have done. Please allow me to show you one of my solid, tangible works…"

While I crossed the room, I remarked with some surprise that the floor was subtly moving. It was as if I had suddenly found myself within a delicately-woven dream. I had to make a huge effort to reach the bookshelves and look for the volume that Hilario had covered with his insulting annotations. I was sure that I had left it in the middle of one of the shelves and began to hunt hazily through the books, pulling out copy after copy, but under the effect of the mirage I could not find my own. It was nowhere to be seen. After an infuriating and fruitless search, I was suddenly overcome by the terrible feeling that I was somehow *losing my solidity*. It was as though *the sole proof of my existence* had been reduced to that small green book whose cover bore my name… I felt faint and hurried to the window; the smell of paper pulp seemed already to be oozing from my hands. When I threw open the window, the warm, dark night air filled my lungs and the visible world began to settle once more into peaceful immobility.

"Hilario must have hidden the book while he was looking for the bottle of wine," I stammered as I emerged from my daze.

"It is all *Hilaguio*'s fault," Emma fired back from the far end of the room.

"I should never have come to this house…"

"Do you want to go back to the city?"

"I think it's a good idea," I admitted, somewhat reassured by the undeniable density of my body.

"Take me with you!" she whispered, as if fearful of an eavesdropper behind the curtains.

"I can't. I didn't even bring my car."

She moved a few paces to the drinks cabinet, squeezed two fingers into the gap near the wall and pulled out a set of keys.

"These are *Hilaguio*'s car keys," she said.

Everything seemed to be falling into place, as in a fantastic melodrama.

"Do you really want us to steal that pile of scrap?" I asked. "Hilario will come down as soon as we start the engine."

"We can lock the door."

"You should go alone. I'll try to keep him in the house."

"But I do not know how to drive that horrid machine," she replied, pressing the keys into my hand.

She now seemed animated by a sudden burst of energy and, for an instant, I pictured the pair of us racing through the shadowy deserts of Castile. I even smiled at the thought of our flight inspiring the amusing headline:

MAN FLEES FRIEND'S HOUSE WITH CAR AND WIFE.

It was beyond ridiculous, of course; the drama would end as soon as we left the garden. The real authors of the farce were surely hiding behind a wall, ready to gloat over their triumph amidst applause and laughter: my friends from the literary *tertulia*, perhaps, or a journalist trying to enliven August's silly season.

"Why don't I come and get you tomorrow?" I said, squinting outside and seeing nothing.

"No, not tomorrow, now! Let's leave now!" she implored, pressing her shivering body (so full of promise!) against me. "What are you afraid of?"

"Of you, I suppose," I replied.

"I think that you're afraid of *Hilaguio*."

"Afraid of that imbecile? Of course I'm not."

I believe that this was when she understood that she would obtain nothing by this approach, because she then abruptly changed tack. She forced me to turn and look her straight in the eye.

"Don't you want to kiss me anymore?" she purred.

My confusion deepened, and I wondered whether this woman was indeed looking for a way out of Hilario Campillo's deranged clutches. The idea cannot have worried me for long, because I set about playing the part expected of me – that of romantic hero – and began to kiss her violently. Our lips met like two magnets, and I felt as though I were diving into a roiling, broiling sea. It was as if the excitement that had built over the course of the evening had suddenly boiled up in the very centre of my being, covering my skin in a dew of feverish sweat. I had never felt so electrified at someone's trembling touch. I was so stupefied at the intensity of our kiss that I wondered if my host could have added some libidinous stimulant to the wine.

This time, she didn't resist when my hands began to wander over the curves of her body. When I traced the delicious outline of her breasts, I noticed that she too was abandoning herself to the whirlwind of our embrace: she was sighing, groaning and murmuring incomprehensible scraps of phrases, opening her eyes from time to time as though to check that I hadn't disappeared from her arms. The time had come to choose a place for our carnal surrender—the enormous sofa or the warm shadows of the garden. The former seemed more suitable; the latter, less exposed. I opted for the garden. (I still had to consider the possibility of Hilario, regretting the whole vengeful scheme, bursting in with criminal intent). I pushed her towards the garden door, the manoeuvre a masterful mixture of slow rocking steps and unexpected waltzing spins. She let herself be carried away, like the survivor of a shipwreck. At that moment, she probably no longer cared that I didn't believe a single word of the whole *mise en scène*. I remember the feeling of her fingernails in my back, my tongue trembling a sweet tremolo between her teeth and my hands plucking, one by one, all the secret strings of her body. We had almost reached the door when, pushed by I know not what audacious curiosity, I asked her *real* name.

"Emma…" she answered vaguely, as though treading water, rocked by waves and ocean winds.

"Call me Leon, if you like," I crooned, disposed to go along with the heady role-play.

Her eyes flew open and she glared at me. She seemed to have shot to the surface of the waves, as though having realised at the last minute that she was going to be swallowed up by the deep.

"Still you mock me!" she exclaimed, trying to free herself from my embrace.

"No, no…" I hastened to make amends (what had possessed me to ask her name at such a moment?) "You're mistaken. I only—"

"You wretch!" she spat at me through gritted teeth.

"Emma, Emma…" I whispered insincerely in her ear.

"Let me go!"

We struggled in silence for a few seconds, like a pair of Greco-Roman wrestlers executing a complicated move. I soon had her immobilised, her back to me; prey to the flames of lust, I held her firmly by the waist. We were near a window and her gaze was drawn upwards to the cold glimmer of the stars. She spoke, her tone one of high drama:

"Whence comes this insufficiency in life—this instantaneous turning to decay of everything on which I lean?"

Once more, I recognised the words of Flaubert, but I kept my mouth shut. I was sure that only by accepting her fantasy would I manage to satisfy my lubricious desires.

"When all is said and done," she continued, pursuing her descent from ecstasy to melancholy, "no one ever wishes to help us. That's the truth."

"But I can help you, Emma…" I whispered again, holding her body tightly against my own and inhaling again that vegetable odour, the smell of forests, budding leaves or freshly-sawn wood.

"I cannot trust you anymore," she said, her charming shoulders drooping with discouragement.

"Of course, you can. We'll start that car and we'll run far away from here," I replied, less concerned by the foolish prospect of flight than by the slow and delightful resurrection that the touch of her body was provoking in my own.

"Did you know that I've already thought of putting an end to my misery?"

"Well, obviously!" I replied like an imbecile, my every sense thrilling at our proximity.

"What do you mean?"

"Nothing," I said, suddenly worried that I might say too much and reveal to Charles Bovary's wife her tragic end. "I mean... I've also thought of it."

"Unfortunately, characters like us cannot take certain decisions without written instruction."

"I see," I replied. I was at present determined to reach my solitary ecstasy by any shameful means necessary.

There was a brief silence, then she turned to face me, her profile quizzical (and, having noticed my febrile tumescence, somewhat abashed).

"You really wish to help me?"

"Yes!"

"But you still believe not a word of my story."

"I believe you! I do!"

"No, no, you refuse to accept the obvious," she insisted, suddenly trying to duck out of my arms. "I'm going to give you conclusive proof."

"I don't need any proof," I replied, continuing my amorous assault, by now determined to accept any explanation as long as it would permit me to reach my goal.[5]

"Let me go, I beg you," she cried. She began to struggle, and I was overcome by a wave of anguish. This must have distracted me, and before I knew it she was out of my arms, leaving me paralysed and panting at the

---

[5] This episode will perhaps scandalise readers familiar with Germán Altabella's prudish literary style. However, those of us who know him will grant that the aggressive, obscene behaviour described in these pages is not completely out of character. (Note: Mario Pallochi)

gates of Paradise. From behind the sofa I saw her smile at me teasingly, as though she knew the terrible state she was leaving me in.

"Come back here, Emma!" I begged her, darting towards her, my arms outstretched, as ridiculous and grave as Dr Frankenstein's creature.

"No, I have to show you the proof," she retorted, nimbly circling the armchairs to avoid my rapacious clutches.

This surreal chase around the room continued for a moment or two, but then the insidious rocking sensation of earlier returned and I was forced to sit on the sofa, temporarily abandoning my impassioned pursuit. She stood behind me and stroked my hair prudently; then she turned and disappeared through the curtains, leaving me alone on the deck of a fragile, listing ship.

NINE

I closed my eyes, trying to neutralise the effects of the tide, but the darkness made it worse: a furious cyclone, or hurricane, seemed to be shaking the house to its foundations. I decided to focus on the steadily-rocking bookcase, all the while telling myself that three glasses of wine alone could not be responsible for my sudden, vertiginous plunge into wanton madness. Even if my spirit was troubled by the oscillating, sinuous reality before me, it nourished but one hope, one goal: to possess that elusive young woman who vacillated so perversely between abandon and resistance. Hilario's potion seemed to affect the other objects in the living room; the piano's yellow smile and the complacently-nodding stripes of the wallpaper were naught but salacious *voyeurs*, encouraging me to pursue my obscene project.[6] In my state of lascivious exaltation, I felt no curiosity about the 'irrefutable proof' that the young woman had wished to show me. Every cell in my body, the very *pneumas* of my soul were fixated on conquering

---

[6] For the commentator of this manuscript, the "potion" hypothesis is hardly necessary. (Note: Mario Pallochi)

the delicate curves that I had so clumsily stroked a few minutes earlier.

I remained stretched out on the sofa, waiting for the floorboards to stabilise and the wallpaper stripes to cease their serpentine undulation. Twice I tried to visualise my route back to the city, attempting to undo the journey from the café and that grotesque interview that was soon to change my life forever... To no avail. I couldn't tear my mind from the quivering body of that young woman, and I imagined the delicacy and dexterity with which I would kiss her neck and ears before we both fell into a bottomless chasm of lust... I was already there, in my fantasy, when I suddenly felt a pressing need, no doubt due to the glasses of Rioja. I decided to step into the garden. (Too risky to wander the dark corridors of the house in search of the facilities.) I stood up and, avoiding the needlish swaying of the coffee table and the barefaced assault of the armchair, I opened the door. The night's warm belly closed around me.

It took me a while to discern the imprecise silhouette of the trees. I regret that I am unable to tell the reader to which species they belonged; the absence of light and the nebulous state of my consciousness prevented any taxonomical examination. I only remember relieving myself against the ruddy bark of a trunk and thinking of the ignoble deluge as my revenge against the insulting annotations that Hilario had scribbled in my novel.

Turning back to the house, I noticed a light in one of the first-floor windows. Picking my way through the darkness, I advanced a few metres and contemplated for the last time Hilario Campillo's distinctive silhouette. His hand propping his chin, he appeared to be reading or writing on a small table that I couldn't see from the garden. Perhaps he was musing over the act of betrayal that the young woman and I were soon to commit. Trembling, anguished, I suddenly thought of the poor libertine's ill-fortune, and an inexorable tenderness plucked at my alcohol-soaked heartstrings. I must have been a real cad to take part in such a cruel act of vengeance... I felt my eyes filling with tears. I wanted to hug him, to implore him not to hold it against me. Like a surgeon trying to reassure the patient on his operating table, I wanted to promise him that the procedure would be simple and painless... My spirit was so crushed by the weight of my guilt that I had to fight the urge to fall on my knees and mutely beg his forgiveness.

I heard a whisper from the evanescent creature: "*Where are you?*" Immediately, every last heady urge stirred up by Hilario's potion reawakened, tearing me from my contrition. At present a depraved, ferocious ogre, I strode through the trees and found my victim on the narrow gravel path leading to the door. The light spilling from the house barely touched her body. She had changed into a long dress with wide puffed sleeves, decorated with layered frills and flounces, as well as an enormous hat which cast a bluish shadow over her eyes. I stopped, confused, a few feet from the deliciously anachronistic figure. Hilario and his wife surely imagined Madame Bovary thus; admittedly, she had that same Andalusian-aristocrat air as on the day of her fevered excursion with Leon. She was so ridiculous, so artificial, in her nineteenth-century regalia! Were they hoping that this disguise would convince me that she really was Flaubert's heroine? I briefly tried to imagine her in that mysterious carriage hurtling through the streets of Rouen, romping with the young clerk…

"I was afraid that you had left!" she exclaimed guardedly, her voice shaking.

"As if I would have left you on your own!" I replied. I came a few steps closer, ready to tug at ribbons, to rip off buttons in my haste to possess her body, itself ever more distant and out of reach. (One must not forget that at this late hour, such an ensemble had something of a perverse, erotic charge to it; those layered skirts, flounces and frills were but exciting obstacles in our game.)

"Now, do you believe me?" she asked, letting the veil of her hat fall over her eyes, plunging her face into a discomfiting blackness.

"You're the heroine of my dreams—the one and only Emma Bovary," I replied hypocritically, in syrupy French.

I know not if she detected the irony in my words; in any case, she said nothing to make me think so. I eagerly wrapped my arms around her waist and held her tightly. The light, fluttering veil irritated me: the maddening hostility of objects! I tore off her hat with something akin to violence and her hair cascaded over her shoulders. Against the moonlight, her face suddenly resembled a fascinating romantic engraving, imbued with the mysterious splendour of yore. But to my excited, lustful eyes, the time for romance had passed. In the middle of the path, we made too visible a tableau; I gently pushed her to the side.

"No, no—we must leave now!" she said, trying to resist.

I pretended not to have heard her and carried her in my arms towards the trees. There, I kissed her neck and, purring, nibbled on her delicate ears now veiled by glossy black hair. She began to pant like one of the actors in those obscene German films I so often watched on TV. But she was as yet unwilling to give herself up to my urgent embrace.

"We must leave… we must leave…" she repeated, struggling to separate herself from my hands, my kisses.

Alas, it was too late to stop my ardent, impetuous advances! My whole body was flooded by a torrent of black lust, gushing through toes, teeth and lips. I pushed her against a tree trunk. She gesticulated a moment, trying to escape, but I held her firmly and continued to kiss her.

"*Non! Non! Hilaguio—Hilaguio!*" she cried suddenly in her outlandish accent.

If she was calling for help, mustn't I have been mistaken in my hypothesis? I wondered as I clawed the first flounce from her skirts. By now, it was all the same to me: whether a hoax, cruel act of vengeance, or even a prank mounted by a rakish husband or lover of pastiche, I couldn't have cared less. No longer did I worry about microphones hidden in the branches of the trees. It was as though the boundless momentum that propelled me had ripped the pair of us from the Earth's surface and dropped us somewhere distant and elastic, like a gigantic spider's web. And there in the centre of it, screaming and fighting – or ceding, for a second or two, to my savage appetite – was the prey who, all night, had tempted me with those black, flashing eyes. The master of the house could not *not* have heard the cries from the first-floor bedroom, but I failed even to ask myself why he did not come to her rescue—why he didn't come to finish me off. My ogreish mind had but one obsession: that of finding a path, a passage or a fissure in her skirts and laces, which now stood as a fortified wall to my clumsy hands. By good fortune, after a few minutes – those few minutes could have been seconds or centuries to my addled mind – she stopped struggling and began to cry out *oui, oui, ouiii!* in such varied and delicious tones that her assailant almost ceased his attack. He had not yet broken through the outer walls of the fortress; he was still battling with corset strings in his fanciful desire to uncover a body up as yet only known by touch and imagination.

The siege would doubtless have continued for a long time if she hadn't (gently but firmly) made me change tactics by turning around and showing me, indirectly and with great delicacy, to which front I should send my scouts. I remember that before undertaking the final assault, I gazed for a moment at her fine silhouette, enlaced with that of the tree – she was so much more desirable and fascinating than my nightly parade of shapely *Hausfraus* on satellite television – then I squeezed her against me and let my hands rummage among her voluminous petticoats, lewdly blazing a trail that would allow me to bring my invasion to a definitive conclusion.

[At this point in my recollections, I sheepishly feel that I must make a point regarding the unexpected *dénouement* of my tale. Not because of the obscene turn taken—those who know me know that I would never dare speak of such things if these events did not hold the key to my tragic disappearance. I have other reasons. Namely, I would like to warn the reader that the story is on the point of slipping into a genre that I have always judged unworthy of universal literature. I refer, of course, to the fantastic: those odious flights of fancy that, by their sheer stupidity, bastardise short stories and novels alike. Unfortunately for me, the implausible happenings of the 7th August were soon to culminate in one of those occurrences, quite beyond all credence, which I would previously have seen as the fruit of a disturbed authorly mind. (However, what happened that day proved to me – in a very singular way, admittedly –

the surprising *reality* of fantasy.) So, impelled by the noble desire scrupulously to record the facts, I must now commit the same folly as those upon whom I have so often derided in my articles and during literary *tertulias*. I hope that the reader, *thus warned*, will not hate me. I have sometimes thought that Hilario Campillo intended, as part of his vengeance – if vengeance it was – to oblige me to conclude my account with a jarring U-turn, which some would wrongly interpret as a damning absurdity on my part.]

As I have already said, that night in the garden I pressed myself against the young woman's body while she pressed herself against the tree; I let my hands explore the strategic (and providential) unlocked gate of the fortress. I have only a confused memory of the rest. Not for want of trying – I've gone over that night hundreds of times – but because everything appeared to happen at the same time, in a simultaneous paroxysm of sensations. That of the jubilant union of our two bodies, yes; but then we began to be shaken by other feelings, troubling and strange. These came not, as I had first thought, from the young woman's delicious spasms, but invaded my enfeebled senses like a sudden deluge brought on by a terrible storm. The whole planet appeared to be moving: branches swung, the air whirled around us and the earth trembled beneath our feet while above our heads the stars tried to return to their positions, as though imprisoned by a powerful magnetic field. A deafening hullabaloo accompanied the gigantic palpitation, its roars matching the rhythm of the young woman's trembling breaths. Stunned by the tectonic shift, I continued my salacious back-and-forth, not daring to modify my rhythm for fear that a tree would fall on us. (As far as I could recall, my lovemaking had never known such turbulence). I do not know how long all this lasted; time itself appeared to have lost its cyclical stability. Nor do I know when the seismic din transformed into the rumble of carriage wheels, or at what moment the clacking of horses' hooves against cobbles became audible, or what provoked our staggering fall. *Fall* is surely a term too bland to convey the miracle; perhaps it could be better described as a powerful vacuum, where there was neither *up* nor *down*, *far* nor *near*, *before* nor *after*. If I speak of a *fall*, it is only to evoke the vertigo that assailed my consciousness at the precise instant when the solitary shadows surrounding us suddenly opened to reveal a different, unknown landscape. We had fallen to the bottom of a well, expecting sudden death, only to find ourselves *on the other side*. And this hinterland was a dark, enclosed space, cracking and groaning with the clatter of horses and squeak of springs. Discoloured, sun-scorched curtains hid what must have been openings to the outside; within was a jolting, stuffy compartment, evidently designed to go backwards and forwards on a paved road. When I describe it now, I perhaps give the impression that I was in possession of all my faculties—that I was able to recognise the noise of hooves and the shape of the cab. Reader, I was far from this: every detail came to me in the most confusing manner.

Crushed beneath an avalanche of new sensations, I was naught but a poor victim attempting to place himself in the universe. Before me, the young woman continued to groan, arching her back as though the staggering dissolution of Hilario's garden were not enough to interrupt our joyful fornication; behind us, shirtless and glistening with sweat, a young blond man with a thick moustache was staring at me in mute horror. You have surely guessed, reader, that I was inside a carriage—the self-same conveyance from which Emma Bovary had been snatched by Hilario Campillo's diabolical pen. It took me a little while to reach this conclusion, for the situation was delicate and I had but one priority: to cut short our obscene copulation and hide my private parts from the man gazing at me, open-mouthed, from the back of the compartment (*he too*, I noticed, was trying to readjust his silly white trousers).

Having finally guessed the identity of the young man and our new location, I felt like an enormous, repugnant insect on the icing of a cake. All was so tragically real (and at the same time so lamentably prosaic and definitive) that my strange evening with Hilario seemed but part of a fantastic nightmare.

"*Mais qu'est-ce que c'est...*" roared the clerk once he had pulled his trousers up.

Hearing his words, the young woman stopped the furious rocking of her hips, turned and gazed at both of us with indescribable perplexity.

"Ohhh...!" she exclaimed, the back of her left hand covering her mouth in the delightfully dramatic manner of romantic heroines.

I underwent a sudden revelation, and realised that, in a sense, this strange little woman *had to be* Emma Bovary. But of course, it was far too late. I would have liked to ask her to explain her prodigious reincarnation, but the young Leon grabbed me by the neck and pushed me to one side of the car with a vigour uncommon in a clerk. At first, I didn't attempt to resist—I was, after all, an intruder in a space into which even Flaubert had not dared to peep. When he kicked open the door, I thought that the cabman would stop the vehicle. He did not. I remember that we were going down an empty street, flooded with intense sunlight; I clung onto the seat, the pale curtains and then the handle of the door (swinging backwards and forwards with each violent jolt of the carriage) while Leon forced me to let go of each anchor with the same pitiless cruelty that would rear its head upon the abandonment of his pitiful mistress a few months later. He pushed me one last time, sending me toppling headfirst into the street. I would like to believe that, after my rough landing, I heard a woman's cry echoing behind me... But perhaps it was myself, howling at the prospect of my dreadful fate, trapped in a world that was not mine.

TEN

As one lost in a thick fog, I opened my eyes many hours later to two distant but terrifying white-horned faces who, leaning towards me out of the mist, were trying to tell me something. I understood but one word: *monsieur*.

Over the course of the next few days, I emerged slowly and with great difficulty from a persistent haze, and discovered that the horned monsters were, in fact, nuns, who bustled silently around the beds in a large dormitory. Very quickly, I also recognised my hands, inert body and head swathed in bandages, and I was able to wander back through the shadowy corridors of memory to that fateful 7th August, which now seemed very distant, as though obscured by clouds of dust. One of the sisters informed me that the month was indeed August, but that of the year 1855. I learnt the news without a murmur, for that very idea, lumpish and menacing, had been looming at the back of my mind for a while. Nor were any questions necessary to establish that I was in an old Rouen hospital. I accepted my new situation far more easily than even I would have expected, and my befuddled spirit's first regret was not the fact of being one hundred and thirty-nine years behind my contemporaries, but that of not having read more of those loathsome fantasy novels, in order to learn how one gets by after being propelled, without money and without resources, into another century. My natural prudence and distrust kept me from telling the doctors the real reason for my presence in their city. Instead I claimed that I had fled Spain for political reasons. There is nothing more compromising, nor more dangerous, than leading people to doubt our sanity; Heaven only knows how long I would have been confined to that sinister hospital had I insisted on giving an authentic version of the facts.

I will spare the reader all the old-fashioned treatments to which I was subjected—by all accounts, so much time had passed between my unfortunate *accident* and admission to the hospital that the doctors had feared for my life. Needless to say, my convalescence was long and tedious; had it not been for the attentions of a charitable widow who came each day to visit the sick, I doubt I would have pulled through. Over these few months, I had ample time to muse on the marvel and to fret about my uncertain future. As for the miracle, I concluded that Hilario had not foreseen my sudden transport through the centuries, that he had probably been every bit as surprised as I to find his house and garden deserted, and my disappearance reported in the papers. Given that his diabolical experiments only worked at moments of frantic copulation, I deduced that I had been a mere wanton instrument for returning Emma to her mysterious literary universe. I could not identify the dark forces that had projected me, with her, into a strange land and time, but I believe that Hilario Campillo had sought *uniquely* to rid himself of Flaubert's heroine, who had become a great burden to him, incompatible with his obscene intention of possessing Nabokov's nymphet. (The symbolic weight of such a substitution might interest a specialist.)

As to my unclear future in that picturesque Norman city, the reader can but imagine how helpless we men of letters feel in such a delicate, anachronistic situation. You may imagine that the author of this tale put to use his knowledge of the great scientific advances of the twentieth century. But what does anyone really know of such things? I had never understood the mechanism of telephones and televisions; obviously I would never have managed to recreate one. I regretted my lack of schooling in French history, for any erudition in that area would have allowed me to pass into posterity as a great prophet. As it was, I had to limit my 'predictions' to a handful of late-century colonial wars and the construction of a monstrous metal tower in the heart of Paris. I do not think that either of these predictions would have sufficed to cover my most urgent expenses. I even renounced the idea of recounting my extraordinary adventure in a novel, convinced that no editor would agree to publish a tale so far-fetched and immoral. In any case, my being a Spaniard made people suspect me of having an overactive imagination—this was, after all, a country characterised at the time by an implacable positivism. I had no recourse but to throw myself on the mercy of the devoted widow who came to visit us (and who, it seemed to all appearances, had inherited from her late husband a discreet but solid fortune). I had to use all my powers of flattery and seduction for the few minutes that she accorded me each day. As her visits became longer and longer, I was able to establish – as with a very precise thermometer – the growing esteem that, little by little, I was rousing in her compassionate breast.

A handsome fellow, convalescent in the bed next to mine, seemed also to fix his gaze – and, perhaps, his future too – on the same lady, and I saw no other solution to his presence but an innocent lie: he was transferred, at my request, to the contagious ward, where the widow rarely dallied. This delicate manoeuvre cost me a possession admired and coveted by nurses and doctors alike: my old wristwatch.

When I was finally able to get out of bed, the widow would accompany me on my daily walks around the sunny garden. That was where I kissed her for the first time; it was there too, we might say, that she decided to marry the Castilian *hidalgo* who had fled his country for reasons that were noble, if a little obscure. I later learnt that what had warmed her to me was my Spanish accent and my traditional, conservative mind-set—*"a little old-fashioned, to tell the truth."* As in fairy tales, after the wedding I took possession of the princess and her treasures and, after a few months, I was so happy with my situation that the forty-five years of my future-past seemed to me naught but the product of an absurd hallucination. I must say, however, that whenever we made love in our fifteen-room manor house (the number of rooms almost matched by the number of servants within), I was sometimes tormented by the thought of Hilario Campillo choosing such a moment to 'bring me home' to the twentieth century. But I was not a character in a novel, and the threat of once again having to scrape a living from newspaper articles and French lessons became ever more distant.

Sometime later, I discovered a copy of *Madame Bovary* in a bookshop. It was, of course, a first edition and I rushed to buy it, as though I still believed that I would one day show it to the members of my literary circle. I realised that, at the time of my arrival in Rouen, Flaubert must have been working on the third part of his novel—that of the well-known 'carriage' episode. I wished to visit the famous wordsmith, to tell him of my adventure, but I did not, fearing that he would reveal that I was nothing more than a product of his imagination, a piece of nonsense that had traversed his consciousness during a high fever, for instance, or terrible nightmare.

In fact, only once did I speak to anyone of the turbulent century of my birth: in 1861, after a dinner party in Paris. We were the guests of my wife's relations, prosperous bankers. After the meal, while the other invitees were smoking enormous cigars and planning audacious business ventures, I spent a moment exploring the quiet corners of the house and soon found myself in a large library, filled with luxurious leather-bound volumes. A young man, ferreting among the shelves, did not even turn around when he heard me enter the room. Stepping forward, I quickly recognised him as one of the other guests. I knew not his name, but someone had told me that he was a stockbroker and had mounted, with mixed success, two or three plays in a Parisian theatre. I recall that he had a fine, manly face, and a profound, intelligent look in his eyes. As he seemed little disposed to conversation, I joined him in looking at the books. However, a few minutes later, the young man turned to show me, with naïve enthusiasm, a small book recounting some experiments with dirigibles. I could not stop myself from smiling, thinking that I was probably not the best person to impress with balloon flights. I assured him, nevertheless, that in due course such vessels would appear slow and dangerous and that they had little future. He was, of course, greatly surprised by my prediction and asked me if I was an expert on the topic. I replied that I was, in a manner of speaking. The man wished to hear my ideas for the future of mankind, and I spoke to him of aeroplanes, atomic submarines and spy satellites. The delicious Burgundy that we had drunk with the meal was doubtless responsible for my startling prolixity as I described helicopters, television and missions to the moon. I believe that any other man would have taken me for a lunatic, but not this one: he invited me to sit in an armchair and began scribbling down everything I said. He was visibly impressed and could not understand how I had imagined such things. What surprised him the most was the certitude with which I paraded before his nineteenth-century eyes all the wonders of the twentieth. Obviously, I was unable to tell him how anything actually worked... When the rest of the party thundered into the library, my companion seemed annoyed and wanted to know if we could see each other the following day. Alas, my wife and I were due to return to Rouen. The man gave me his visiting card and asked me to drop by if ever I was in Paris. I slipped it into my pocket and moved quickly away from him, worried that he might say something that would make the other honourable guests doubt my mental state. That night, in the hotel, I glanced at the card. Printed in the middle, beside an address long since forgotten, was a familiar name: *Jules Verne*. I let out a cry upon realising that my careless talk had just contributed, definitively and irredeemably, to the birth of science fiction. (I must add that, years later, when Verne began to publish his famous novels, I took great pleasure in seeing the ridiculous and timorous way in which he had interpreted my words. His spaceship was but a cannonball and the aerodynamic helicopter that I had described in such detail was transformed into a heavy wooden embarkation, kept airborne by dozens of propellers. Beyond this, he had been afraid to take my fanciful ideas any further.)

Naturally, I never even considered visiting him.

I must not finish this tale without adding a few thoughts on the man who sent me into this strange century and land, which have since become my own. While I have no idea as to what extremes his disturbing reincarnations might have led, I consider him the victim of his own experiments—a sort of tormented and imprudent sorcerer's apprentice. As such, from the shadows of the past I beg that no legal action be taken against him. No one can say whether the author of these lines would have been happier in his native century. One could say that, in an age threatened by nuclear power plants, traffic pollution and pale imitations of rock-and-roll, a life as happy or as peaceful would have been hard to achieve.

Whether in one century or another, Time slowly destroys its passengers. The passionate writer, sharp-sighted critic and respected local hero has become a docile old man who speaks with difficulty and whose gaze still falls upon the streets of this provincial French city with astonishment and disbelief. As one might expect, for many years I have been obsessed by the desire to transmit my story to my former countrymen. Faced with the impossibility of retracing my steps through the mysterious black hole of that fateful night, I had no option but to reconcile myself to a daunting one-hundred-year wait. At first, I had planned to consign the details of my disappearance to white writing-paper, but I quickly realised that such an approach would endanger my fragile manuscript. Who knows how many housewives, how many dim-witted servants might feel the urge to throw a wad of dirty, dusty papers into the fire! I therefore decided to use the pages of a book likely to inspire the respect of future owners and acquired a handsome edition of Grew's *Anatomy of Plants*; the blank backs of the volume's numerous colour plates provided me with enough space to scratch out, in a hand now clumsy and trembling, my account of this astonishing shift of century. Some family friends (wholly ignorant of Spanish), have offered to house this book in their library. As they have many children and grandchildren, I hope that, one hundred years from now, one of their descendants will leaf through *Anatomy of Plants* and, following my urgent instructions, in August 1994 will forward this book to my great friend Mario Pallochi. I know that he will do his utmost to have it published, in deference to the warm friendship that once united us and which, contrary to the way of things, was never blighted by those foolish jealousies so often seen among men of letters. Any royalties from the publication of this story should be directed to him, and with them the undying gratitude of an old man fortunate enough to have lived in two worlds.

Germán Altabella,
Rouen, December 1884

EDITOR'S ADDENDUM

When this book had already gone to press, several new and terrible revelations were made regarding Germán Altabella's disappearance. A hunter chasing a partridge near Villanueva de Vivar – a small village a dozen kilometres from our city – discovered, half-buried between tuffets of grass, the body of our unfortunate subject. It seems that wild animals had uncovered the remains, carefully concealed by the killer. Understandably, this macabre discovery horrified everyone, especially those of us who had admired the illustrious critic and novelist. The enquiry was swiftly stepped up, and the police think they have finally identified the guilty party. It just so happens that the body was found less than 200 yards from the home of a certain Mario Pallochi, the man responsible for preparing this book for publication after having allegedly been sent Germán Altabella's manuscript.

As might be expected, these discoveries raised serious doubts as to the identity of the author of said manuscript. Inspector Ceballos is leaning towards Mario Pallochi, especially since a sharp-eyed proof-reader spotted that the letters making up his name and that of Hilario Campillo are almost the same. Not to mention that using such an absurd, crazy story to explain the victim's disappearance could only be the work of a disturbed, psychopathic writer.

Pallochi, an Argentinian of Italian extraction, had only been living in our area for seven years. He had been working as a publicity agent and had lived for a while in an old house in Villanueva de Vivar. In 1990, he self-published an enormous, unreadable novel – a pale imitation of García Márquez – and had just finished writing another, every bit as bad as the first, which was rejected by our publishing review panel a few months ago. Pallochi seems to us the epitome of a 'frustrated writer', eaten up by secret ambition and pride. Altabella had written in the newspapers a compassionate, ironic critique of Pallochi's first novel. Was his verdict on the second manuscript the motive behind this inexplicable crime? We will have to wait for the murderer's arrest to confirm our suspicions, but for the time being he is nowhere to be found.

Sadly, only now can we see the author's sick, libellous purpose, and finally understand why Germán Altabella comes across as a lewd and brutal man, prepared to go to any lengths in order to get what he wants. Obviously, our late lamented colleague's personality was nothing like that described in these pages, and the reader should rest assured that if it had not already gone to print, this book would never have been published.

We hope that the author of this text will soon be brought to justice. He is nothing more than a vulgar murderer whose arrogance could not resist the temptation of appearing, under a sinister anagram, in this false and slanderous tale.

ACKNOWLEDGEMENTS

My thanks to Lorna Hanwell for her helpful notes and comments during the translation of this novel.

Lightning Source UK Ltd.
Milton Keynes UK
UKHW011403230719
346676UK00001B/83/P